"I'm flying. I swear I'm flying!" Sam thought giddily.

She wanted to go further and further, and he led her into even more complex moves. Then, at the very end, he lifted her off the ground and spun her over his head. The number ended with X's arms fully extended, Sam eight feet off the ground, and her wild red hair spilling like a waterfall toward the floor.

The place went totally wild.

This is what I'm meant to do! Sam realized, her heart pounding with adrenaline. *And this is the guy* I'm meant to do it with!

Sunset Touch

CHERIE BENNETT

Sunset™
Island

SPLASH™

B

A BERKLEY / SPLASH BOOK

SUNSET TOUCH is an original publication of
The Berkley Publishing Corporation. This work
has never appeared before in book form.

SUNSET TOUCH

A Berkley Book / published by arrangement with
General Licensing Company, Inc.

PRINTING HISTORY
Berkley edition / October 1993

A GLC BOOK

Splash and *Sunset Island* are trademarks belonging to
General Licensing Company, Inc.

ISBN: 0-425-13708-2

BERKLEY®
Berkley Books are published by The Berkley Publishing Group,
200 Madison Avenue, New York, New York 10016.
BERKLEY and the "B" design
are trademarks belonging to Berkley Publishing Corporation.

PRINTED IN THE UNITED STATES OF AMERICA

10 9 8 7 6 5 4 3 2 1

for Suburban Man

ONE

Yes, indeedy and whoa, baby! Samantha Bridges said to herself, looking around the green room of Portland, Maine's Downeast Sound Studios. *This is the big time!* She looked over at her best friend, Emma Cresswell, and grinned happily.

"This is great, isn't it?" Emma whispered to Sam with excitement.

"No more than we deserve, girlfriend," Sam said blithely. She wanted to hug herself, she felt so happy.

"Today is a major, totally major day, girls!" Sheldon Plotkin, the executive from Polimar Records called over to Sam and Emma.

"Absolutely!" Sam called back to him.

The door opened, and the studio engineer, Val Gallay, stuck his head in. "How goes it?"

"Hey, I'm Sheldon Plotkin, Polimar Records—call me Shelly," the short, balding, jean-clad record company exec told the sound engineer.

"You got it, Shelly," Val said, shaking Shelly's proffered hand.

"We're talking mega-group in the studio today," Shelly told Val. "I mean, these kids are major dynamite! Highly flammable! Too hot to handle!" Shelly licked his thumb and punched the air with it, making a sizzling sound.

Sam and Emma stifled their giggles. They'd met Sheldon "Call-Me-Shelly" Plotkin backstage at the final gig Flirting with Danger—or the Flirts, as everyone called them—had performed on their big East Coast tour. They thought Sheldon was a hoot.

"Be nice," Emma whispered to her friend. "Shelly's got clout."

Sam snorted. "I hope so," she shot back, "because that's all he's got."

"Sam!" Emma chastised her, biting her

lip to keep from laughing.

"Why did the poor guy's parents name him Sheldon?" Sam continued in a loud whisper. "I mean, can you imagine having a hot romance with some guy named Sheldon? Ooo, Sheldon! Kiss me, Sheldon! I've never felt anything like this before, Sheldon!"

Emma shook her head, letting the laughter escape from between her lips.

"Just what I figured," Sam whispered. "A guy's mother names him Sheldon, he's gonna turn out bald and lonely!"

"Sam!" Emma reprimanded.

"Okay, okay, I'll behave," Sam grinned, turning to look at the other members of the band, who were all assembled in the green room, and whom Shelly Plotkin was glad-handing mercilessly. Val, in the meantime, had returned to the control room.

While waiting for their recording session to start, Sam was her usual wisecracking, careless self, but inside she was a jumble of emotions. And chief among the emotions was fear. Sam, along with Emma, and the girls' archenemy, Diana De Witt, was one of the Flirts' three backup singer-dancers. And when Sam was honest with herself, she had to admit that she was a much better dancer than singer.

Stop scaring yourself! she admonished, even as she kept up a stream of idle chit-chat with Emma. *This is the studio. If it doesn't turn out right the first time, we'll just do another take. Besides, you look hot.*

Sam believed that whenever you felt your worst, you should dress your best. Knowing that she'd be nervous in the studio, she'd chosen cutoff jeans, and a hot pink bra top under a frayed jean jacket. On her feet she wore her lucky trademark red cowboy boots. She'd brushed her long red hair upside down and made the curls as wild as possible, put on tons of mascara and deep matte-red lipstick. Emma looked great, too, Sam noted. But then, she always did. Emma had on a long white cotton skirt over a white lace leotard, covered by her pink jean jacket. A slender pale pink ribbon held back her perfect blond bob.

"How is it that you always look so perfect?" Sam asked her friend.

"Oh, I wake up at four, five o'clock in the morning to achieve this effect," Emma replied solemnly. She looked around the studio. "Can you believe we're actually here?"

"Yup," Sam replied laconically. "I belong here and you, Oh Ice Princess, belong everywhere. Of course, that leaves out Diana. She belongs in purgatory. Forever."

"Amen," added Emma, who couldn't stand Diana any more than Sam could.

Sam took in the sound booth, the recording studio, and got a little thrill all over again. Actually, she was as amazed as Emma at the events that had brought the two of them to this recording session, and, when she thought about it, at the events that had made her, Emma, and Carrie Alden—who was busy working that night—best friends.

First, they had all met more than a year before at the International Au Pair Convention in New York City, where each was trying to get a summer job. The fact that they had met at all amongst the hundreds of girls trying for jobs was amazing enough. But then, they had all been chosen by families who summered on fabulous Sunset Island, the famous resort island off the coast of Maine. And then, all three had been invited back for the next summer!

Okay, the Jacobs family is a little strange, Sam thought, musing about the precocious fourteen-year-old twins and their single dad. *Okay, a lot strange. But is it any stranger than Emma and Carrie and I becoming best friends? Emma is only a perfect blond heiress from one of the richest families in America. And Carrie, girl-next-door brunette daughter of two pediatricians in New Jersey, is a hotshot photographer and student at Yale. And then there's me. So what if I'm tall, redheaded and incredibly cute? I come from Junction, Kansas, and my life was a total bore before Emma and Carrie were in it! Now I'm a backup singer for one of the hottest up-and-coming bands in the country, and—*

"Can I have all the Flirts over here?" Shelly Plotkin called, breaking into Sam's reverie. He motioned to a couple of couches

on the far side of the green room while simultaneously mopping perspiration from his
brow.

Sam and Emma walked over with
the group. Already seated were long-
haired, gorgeous Billy Sampson, the band's
leader and lead singer (and Carrie's boyfriend); Presley Travis, the sexy guy from
Tennessee who played bass and who was
Sam's on-again-off-again (currently on-
again) boyfriend; Jay Bailey, the mild-
mannered keyboard player; and Sly Smith,
the drummer.

*And there's Diana, sitting as close to Pres
as she can*, Sam noted with narrowed eyes.
*Why does she have to be so gorgeous? Her
outsides deserve to be as ugly as her insides!*

"You're late," Diana said with a sniff, as
Sam sat down on the floor. "Don't be late
coming in on your part."

"Crawl back under your rock, Diana,"
Sam suggested amiably.

Billy stood up and walked over to Shelly.
Sam and Diana knew enough to stop
sniping at each other. He turned and
faced the band.

7

"On behalf of the whole band," Billy began, "I'd like to thank Polimar Records, and especially Shelly here, for believing in us and for bringing us into the studio."

Sam shot a quick look at Shelly, who was beaming like the star on top of a department store Christmas tree.

"Anything you'd like to tell the band, Shelly?" Billy asked the record exec.

Shelly looked startled. "Uh, just that, well, Polimar Records has the greatest confidence in you guys," he managed.

"Great, Shelly, we appreciate that," Billy said.

"And that I firmly believe that this demo tape we're sponsoring for you is going to be the tape that seals a recording contract between your band and our company," Shelly added, getting back his confidence.

"Great, Shelly, we think—"

"And that our relationship is going to set new standards for excellence in the industry," Shelly continued, on a roll. "I mean precedents. Serious precedents."

"Say what?" Sam whispered in Emma's

ear. Emma nudged her in the ribs to be quiet.

"I believe we're gonna, like, mind-meld on this," Shelly continued, his little hands flying through the air. "You guys are beautiful, and—"

"You guys ready?" Val, the engineer, asked, sticking his head into the room. "Shelly?"

Val was also acting as producer on the tape. Polimar had brought him in from Los Angeles for the session, and even Sam knew he had a resume a mile long that included many gold and platinum albums for a variety of artists, and even a couple of Grammy awards.

"They're ready!" Shelly announced, rubbing his hands together in anticipation.

Sam looked at her watch. 7:15 p.m. *As much as I'd like to stay here forever, I hope we don't get out of here too late. I'm supposed to go sailing with the twins tomorrow. Early.*

The band followed Val into the studio, while Shelly settled into the control booth, an expectant look on his face. Billy had

9

briefed the band on how the session was going to run—tonight, they were going to work on two songs. "You Take My Breath Away" and "Love Junkie." Sheldon had picked the tunes out of their repertoire. Billy had written the first one, and Billy and Pres had co-written the second.

"Okay, guys, first we'll lay down the instrumental tracks," Val told them. "Then we'll get the lead vocals, and then you ladies can lay down the backups."

Sam nodded casually. Inside, she didn't feel nearly so confident. *I'm used to us all performing at the same time*, she told herself. *What if I can't even hear my part this way?*

She kept her mouth shut, though, since everyone else seemed to be so confident.

The instrumental tracks for both songs went smoothly. But then the guys had had some experience in the studio. Billy sang his lead vocals, and then it was time for the backups to join in.

"Okay, just slip on the headphones," Val instructed. "The band and lead mix will be coming at you through the phones. It's a rough mix—I'll do the final later."

Sam, Emma, and Carrie each put on a set of earphones and stood in front of a mike.

"You can all sing into the same mike," Val told them. "It'll pick all of you up—it's omnidirectional, just stand close."

"You got it," Diana said confidently, and stepped up to the mike.

"You might want to take the phones off one ear so you can hear yourself," Val suggested. "Okay, ready to go for it?"

The three girls nodded. Sam could feel the perspiration trickling from her armpits.

Fortunately, they started with "You Take My Breath Away"—a love ballad Billy had written for Carrie—which had very simple backup vocals. In fact, all three girls sang "oo" in unison for most of the song. Sam sang confidently, hearing her voice blend well with Emma's and Diana's. They did the tune four times.

"Cool, I think we got that one," Val said from the control booth. "Let's move on to 'Love Junkie.'"

"This one's a killer," Sheldon told Val.

The mike was still on in the control booth and the band heard him.

"Thanks!" Billy called back to Sheldon.

"Really killer, babe!" Sheldon repeated.

"Okay, let's do it!" Val said. "You ladies ready?"

"Ready, willing, and able!" Diana trilled.

"Shut up," Sam mumbled to her with loathing.

"Just try not to wreck this," Diana said coolly.

"Headphones on, girls!" Val called to them.

They put the phones back on and listened intently as the insinuating bass line began, followed by the raucous instrumental and then Billy's lyrics. The girls got ready to come in on their three-part harmony.

Love! Love junkie, baby!
Love! Love junkie, baby!

"Cut!" Val called from the booth. "Uh, who's on melody there?"

"I am," Sam called back to him.

12

"You were singing the high part," Val told her.

"Oh, sorry," Sam said, blushing bright red.

"No big thing, happens to everyone," Val said easily. "You cool now?"

"Oh, sure," Sam replied breezily. She tried to think of her first note. The melody line had completely fled from her mind.

Val played the recording again. Once again, Sam came in on the high part.

"Cut," Val called. "Could someone go over the melody line for her?" he asked from the control room.

"I will," Diana said, clearly disgusted. "It goes like this." She sang Sam's part for her.

"Thanks," Sam said, swallowing her pride.

"Ready to go?" Val asked.

"Ready," Sam assured him.

"Here she comes!" Val called. He ran the tape again.

Sam started singing, and she came in on the right note. *Thank God everything will be okay now*, she thought. But somehow when it got to the high part of the melody she found herself coming in on the same note as Diana, which was a third under where she was supposed to be singing.

"Cut, cut, cut!" Diana yelled, pulling off her earphones. "She's singing my part! I can't work like this!"

"Excuse me, but I think I handle the session," Val called down to Diana.

Diana just threw up her hands in disgust. Sam stared at the floor. Emma reached over and gave her hand a squeeze.

Val came into the studio and took Sam aside.

"I'm really sorry—" Sam began.

"Look, it's no big thing," Val assured her kindly. "A lot of people get freaked the first time they record in the studio."

"I'm not used to singing in the same mike as them," she explained. "When I hear their voices, I just mess up!"

"Okay, so we'll record you separately," Val suggested.

"You can do that?" Sam asked desperately.

"Hey, this is the studio," Val said with

a grin. "We can do anything! Ever hear Madonna live?"

Sam shook her head no.

"Trust me, she can't hit half those notes on her CDs. It's probably all done in the studio!"

"I never knew that," Sam replied.

Val hugged her shoulders kindly. "No sweat." He walked back over to Emma and Diana. "Okay, we're gonna take it this time with just the two of you, then record Sam's part afterward."

"Figures," Diana uttered nastily.

"You got quite a mouth on you," Val told Diana cheerfully.

Diana shot Val the finger.

"Charming," Val commented, heading back to his booth.

"You okay, babe?" Pres asked Sam, coming up to put his arm around her. Sam wearily rested her head on his broad shoulder.

"Your voice fixin' to quit on you?" he drawled in her ear.

"I'm having some trouble hearing the part," Sam admitted, embarrassed.

"Happens to the best of us," Pres comforted her. "Just a question of trainin'."

"My training's in dance, not singing," Sam reminded him.

"That's obvious," Diana called, having overheard Sam's comment.

"Stuff a sock in it," Emma told Diana.

"Ready up here," Val called down to them.

Pres gave Sam a reassuring hug, then went back to the booth. Val ran the tape, and Emma and Diana sang their parts flawlessly.

"Great going," Val called to them. "You ready, Sam?"

"Sure," Sam said, taking a deep breath. Her fists were clenched so tight that she could feel her nails digging into her flesh. *Please let me do this right*, she prayed. *Please don't let me mess it up.*

Love, love junkie, baby!
Love, love junkie, baby!

Sam got through the song. She knew she hadn't sounded particularly good, and her voice hadn't been strong, but thank God

16

she'd basically sung the right notes. After three more takes Val said she was done. Sweat was pouring off her. She excused herself and went to the ladies room to clean up.

Sam stared at her pale, drawn face in the mirror. *I'm a dancer, not a singer!* she protested to her forlorn image in the mirror. All the exciting feelings she'd had just a little while earlier about being in a recording studio had fled from her mind. *What the hell am I doing here, besides making a total idiot out of myself?*

Sam finished reapplying her lipstick and turned to Emma and Carrie. "How's my makeup?" she asked, as they all stood together in the tiny powder room of the Play Café.

It was an hour after the Flirts' recording session had ended, and the band had adjourned to the Play Café, where Emma's boyfriend, Kurt Ackerman, and Carrie Alden were waiting to meet them.

"Fine," Emma assured her.

"You look great," Carrie chimed in.

17

"So do you," Sam said, taking in Carrie's pink overalls with a pink sleeveless T-shirt underneath. "But you'd look even better if we could get some blush on those girl-next-door cheeks of yours!"

Carrie shrugged. "I'm just not much into makeup," she said simply.

"Apparently, Billy doesn't mind," Emma said lightly, defending her friend, and then turned her attention back to Sam. "Look, I wanted to tell you not to pay any attention to Diana—" she continued.

"I don't," Sam shrugged, as she took some mascara out of her small purse. "She's not worth it. Now, let's talk about someone worth paying attention to."

"Pres?" Emma ventured with a teasing grin..

"He's worth it," Sam agreed, "but that's not who I'm talking about."

"Shelly Plotkin?" Carrie joked.

"Perfect for Diana," Sam cracked, "but not my type. Nope, you're both lousy guessers."

"Come on," Carrie said, "they're waiting outside. End the mystery."

"Okay, okay," Sam gave in, putting her makeup away. "Danny Franklin. He called me today."

"You're kidding," Emma responded.

"Nope," Sam replied. "And you'll get to see him in a few days."

"That's great!" Emma said.

"Yeah, I can't wait," Sam agreed.

Sam thought back to how she'd met Danny in Florida, when she'd been a dancer at Disney World. Danny had been her best friend there. Sam often thought he might be kinda, sorta . . . in love with her. But Danny was so shy that it was hard to tell. They had written to each other on and off—or rather, Danny had written to her and she had once or twice managed to actually get a return postcard into the mail—but he was always there, in the back of her mind.

Of course, thinking about Danny reminded her of Disney World, which reminded her that she'd been fired from her dancing job there for being "too original." Well, she wouldn't think about that. She'd just concentrate on Danny.

"He's coming to visit you?" Carrie asked.

"Yep," Sam replied. "He's going on a canoe trip in eastern Maine, and decided to come spend a couple of days visiting little ol' me before he hooks up with his friends in some town called Ellsworth. Can you blame him?"

"What about Pres?" Carrie queried.

"What about him?" Sam answered lightly.

"Does he know?" Emma asked.

"Not yet," Sam admitted.

"What's he going to think?" questioned Carrie.

"Oh, he can stand a little competition," Sam replied. "Besides, I only like Danny as a friend."

That's true, Sam thought to herself. *So far, anyway. Danny's about the most sensitive, interesting guy I've ever met in my life. And I feel like he really cares about me, not just about my looks. And unlike Pres, he did not try to get into my pants.*

"So when are you planning to tell Pres?" Carrie asked.

"I'll call him tomorrow," Sam replied.

"I've had enough excitement for one night in the studio."

"Won't Pres be . . . concerned?" Emma asked.

Sam shrugged, displaying a nonchalance she didn't totally feel. "Hey, it's no biggie. Pres won't mind."

At least I hope not.

TWO

"So?" Emma asked Sam, as Sam plopped down on her new tight-woven brown wicker beach mat.

"Water's fine," Sam said cheerfully, toweling herself off. "Perfect sixty-two degrees, great for Eskimos."

"I don't think Emma's asking about the water," Carrie said, reaching for her tube of sunblock.

"Oh!" Sam said. "My tired voice! All I needed was a good night's sleep—which I got last night because the twins' sailing trip today got canceled—and it's as great as ever."

It was the afternoon after the recording session, and the three girls had managed a couple of hours off to meet at the crowded Sunset Island main beach.

"It's not your singing—"

"Then you must be wondering about the swimsuit!" Sam said, jumping to her feet. "It is sort of wonderful, isn't it?" Sam spun around, showing off the one-piece practically-backless sea-green tanksuit she was wearing.

"Pres, Sam," Carrie prompted her friend, "Pres. And Danny. Pres and Danny?"

"Oh! You're asking about Presley Travis, that babe-alicious Southern guy I'm sometimes seen with," Sam joked.

"Gee, nice that you remember his name," Carrie said. "Did you call him this morning to tell him that Danny Franklin's coming to visit you?"

"Of course I called him," Sam said regally. "Samantha Bridges is a woman of her word."

"So what did he say?" Emma queried.

"Not much," Sam replied.

"Not much?" Carrie repeated.

"He couldn't say much," Sam said truthfully. "I left a message for him on the Flirts' answering machine."

"Sam!" Emma admonished her. "You

can't do that to him. He's your boy-friend!"

"We're not official," Sam said defensively. "Besides, was it my fault he wasn't home for the call?"

Carrie rolled over to give her back some sun, and pulled the straps down from the black maillot she was wearing so she'd tan more evenly. "I guess not," she finally said, skeptically.

"Anyway, I know exactly what he'd say," Sam said. "'You got to make your own choices, so you decide what's best for you sweetheart,'" Sam intoned in a deep-voiced imitation of Pres.

"Well," Emma mused, "he's right, in a way."

"Exactly!" Sam replied, "and I've decided I really want to see Danny. I only like him as a friend, anyway."

"So you said," Carrie responded, looking at Sam skeptically.

"Well, if that's really true there shouldn't be a problem with Pres," said Emma. "Except for what you did on tour—"

"Except nothing," Sam interrupted, turning to look at a gull that was swooping down over the ocean. "What's past is past, right?"

Yeah, right, Sam thought, *I basically ignored Pres during the band's tour, and made a big move for a rock-star-slime-ball who turned out to be secretly-married. Johnny Angel. Major mistake in judgment.*

"So," Carrie asked, "are you looking forward to seeing Danny?"

"Let me tell you something about Danny Franklin," Sam said, leaning forward toward Carrie. "He's the perfect guy . . . for somebody else."

"I thought he looked a little like Tom Cruise," Carrie recalled.

"Yeah, he's seriously cute, huh?" Sam said.

"Hard to believe such a cute guy would be so shy," Emma pointed out.

"Adds to his charm," Sam said. "Remember how I told you he said he was waiting for me to make the first move? Well—"

At that moment, three people—two girls and a guy—approached them, temporarily blocking their sunlight. Sam looked up to see who it was, and groaned.

Diana De Witt, wearing a white thong bikini that showed off her perfectly aerobicized body, stood there with her hands on her hips.

With her was her best friend, Lorell Courtland, the girls' other enemy on the island, wearing a frilly red bikini. Lorell brushed her dark hair back from her face.

"Gee, a great big, fat moon is blocking the sun," Sam said, staring up at her two enemies.

The guy with Diana and Lorell laughed.

I don't recognize him, Sam thought to herself, taking a quick mental inventory of the cute, sandy-haired guy. *About six foot one, about one-ninety. Look at those muscles—he's built like a dancer. Wow, is he in unbelievable shape!*

"Well, aren't you the amusin' one," Lorell trilled, her Georgia accent lilting. "It's amazin' that a girl with your limited brain can be so very clever!"

"Well, she tries, poor thing," Diana said

to Lorell sympathetically.

"Gee, great to see you two," Carrie said, without a note of enthusiasm.

"Resting your voice, Sam?" Diana asked innocently. "Because from how you sounded last night, it could use some rest. Maybe permanent rest, huh?"

"Maybe you could use a permanent fat lip," Sam replied.

"Just joking," Diana said, "no need to be so touchy." She shot a look at the guy between her and Lorell, who was watching the entire scene with a bemused expression on his face.

"Oh!" Diana continued. "How rude of me. Let me introduce our friend to you."

That would be a rare sign of civility, Sam thought. *What a good idea, Diana.*

"Chris," Diana said, taking the guy by the arm, "allow me to introduce you to Samantha Bridges, Carrie Alden, and Emma Cresswell. They work as baby-sitters here on the island."

"Au pairs," Emma corrected Diana.

"Well, same difference," Lorell said with a shrug.

"And this," Diana's grip tightened slightly on the handsome guy's arm, "is Christopher McGriff."

"A pleasure," Emma said, somewhat curtly. Sam and Carrie both nodded to the guy.

"Nice to meet you all," Christopher said, smiling broadly. "My mother did name me Christopher, but if you see me again, you can call me X."

"X?" Sam repeated.

"X," the guy replied, still smiling his winning smile, and aiming his deep blue eyes right at Sam. "Like the letter."

Sam couldn't resist taking a verbal shot at Diana and Lorell's friend. *If he's a friend of theirs, he's not going to be a friend of mine,* she thought. *Even if he is mondo-cute.*

"What's the matter," Sam asked, "you had trouble spelling the name Chris?"

Chris-X laughed. "I was born on Christmas," he explained. "And there's a ton of Chris's out there. So I changed it to X, like in Merry X-mas."

"Yeah, cool," Sam said noncommittally.

She found herself kind of liking X and couldn't figure out what he was doing with the poisonous Diana and Lorell.

"I think we'd better be going now," Lorell said, with a humorless smile.

"Wait a sec," X said, turning back to Sam, Emma, and Carrie. "How do you guys know each other? You don't baby-sit for Lorell and Diana, I presume."

The girls cracked up.

"Not really," Carrie responded. "Emma, Sam, and Diana all sing backup for the same band."

"I see," X smiled. "Well, maybe I'll see you around. I'm teaching some master dance classes at the country club this week. That's where I met Lorell and Diana."

"Hey!" Sam said, "I'm a—"

"Come on," Diana tugged at X's bare arm. "There's some people who are actually interesting that I want you to meet. Over there!" She started dragging X back toward the boardwalk. X waved good-bye.

"Eleven," Sam muttered, when the three of them were out of sight.

"What?" Emma asked.

"Eleven," Sam repeated solemnly. "Eleven on a scale of ten. That guy is a total babe!"

"Stop drooling, Sam," Emma said with a laugh.

"He seemed nice," Carrie said with a shrug.

"I'm telling you, the guy's an eleven," Sam insisted, watching X as he walked across the beach. "And he's a dancer! A dancer and an eleven—be still my fickle heart."

"Uh oh," Carrie grinned, looking at Sam. "I know that look in your eyes."

"What look?" Sam asked innocently.

"The one you've got now," she replied.

"Well," Sam asked, "don't you think so?"

"Think what?"

"That's he's an eleven."

"Sam," Emma said, "you are totally incorrigible."

Sam grinned, lay back down, and turned her face up to the sun. "To know me is to love me!" she said.

Especially if you're a guy dancer, and an eleven.

*   *   *

"So are we gonna meet this Danny guy?" Allie Jacobs asked Sam between forkfuls of spaghetti.

"Yeah," her twin sister Becky added, "or are you afraid we might steal him away from you?"

Sam saw the twins' father, Dan Jacobs, smile good-naturedly at his daughters. "I think Sam can take care of herself," he ventured.

"Well," Becky sniffed, taking a sip of Coke, "everyone thinks we're eighteen, and lots of nineteen-year-old guys go out with eighteen-year-old girls."

It was during a simple dinner that Sam had prepared for the Jacobs twins and their dad that she told them about Danny Franklin's arrival, scheduled for later that night. But even as she described Danny to them, the guy she had met on the beach was on her mind.

"Yeah," Allie agreed. "And we're mature for our age, so that helps."

Sam choked on her spaghetti. "Looking eighteen, acting eighteen, and being eighteen are three totally different things," Sam said, taking a sip of water.

"That's for sure," Allie agreed. "Look at you for example. You're nineteen, and you act twelve."

"Excuse me?" Sam said, looking at Allie.

"You already have a boyfriend," Becky said. "So what are you inviting this Danny here for? That is so un-cool."

Have these girls been consulting with Emma and Carrie?

"When you get older," Sam replied, "you'll see the difference between a boyfriend and just a friend."

"Right!" Dan Jacobs said with too much enthusiasm.

No matter how hard he tries, Sam thought to herself, *he always manages to say the wrong thing.*

"Well," Becky said, "good thing you're gonna be tied up with Danny and Pres. Because I met the cutest new guy today!"

"Yeah, me too," Allie chimed in.

"Tall—"

"Blond—"

"Really handsome—"

"Really really cool—"

"So buff—"

"How old is this fellow?" Dan Jacobs asked with a frown.

"Oh, I don't know," Becky said nonchalantly. "A little older than us, I guess."

Good, Sam thought. *Maybe if Allie gets a real boyfriend she'll calm down a little.*

"Does he have a name?" Dan prompted, wiping his lips with a paper napkin.

Becky and Allie looked at each other.

"Well," Becky said finally, "he does and he doesn't."

"Excuse me?" Dan asked, confused.

"His mother named him Christopher, but he calls himself X!" Allie cried enthusiastically.

X? The twins met X today? Must have been at the club, then.

"Isn't that just the coolest?" Allie rhapsodized. "I'm thinking about changing my name to Y."

How appropriate, Sam thought wryly.

Details about X poured out of the twins like water rushing over a falls. They knew a lot more about him than Sam did, since they'd taken a dance class with him that afternoon, and he'd talked a bit about himself before the class started.

"He's twenty-five—" said Allie.

"And he's already won some prizes—" added Becky.

"For his ballets, and also modern—"

"He lives in Los Angeles—"

"But travels all over the world—"

"Because he's getting so famous—"

"He went to Julliard—"

"But he's here now teaching because—"

"Some big patron lives on the island—"

"But he's the artistic director of—"

"Some big dance company in California—"

"And he's not married and he doesn't have a girlfriend!" the twins fairly shouted together.

"Yeah, like that means you two have a chance," Sam said dryly.

"Girls," Dan said seriously, "don't you think he's a bit old for you?"

"Not!" the twins replied together.

He might be a bit old for them, but not for me, Sam thought involuntarily. Then she tried to banish the thought from her mind. *I already have a boyfriend, and my best friend Danny's arriving later tonight. The last thing I need is yet another guy to think about.*

But try as she might, she couldn't get the image of X standing in front of her on the beach, smiling his easy smile, off her mind. And now she knew that not only was he a dancer, but a great dancer.

Just like me, she thought, *just like me.*

THREE

Sam was singing along with an old Elvis Presley song on the radio at the top of her lungs as Carrie pulled the Templetons' Mercedes into a parking space at the Sunset Ferry terminal. Carrie had offered to drive to the ferry so Sam could concentrate on spotting her old friend. Luckily, Dan Jacobs had said the twins could take care of themselves that evening.

"It's good to give them that freedom now and then, don't you think?" Mr. Jacobs had asked Sam.

"Uh, sure," Sam had agreed, though she didn't trust the twins on their own for two seconds. *Contrary to what the twins think, they are not exactly the most mature fourteen-year-olds on the planet*, Sam thought as she sang along with Elvis.

"Sounds like your voice is fully recovered," Carrie shouted over Sam and the radio.

Sam turned the radio down. "Never better," she grinned, "never better."

"Do you think it means anything that you were just singing 'Heartbreak Hotel'?" Carrie asked, as they waited for the nine o'clock ferry from Portland—carrying Danny Franklin—to pull into the ferryport.

"It's what came on on the oldies station," Sam said with a shrug.

Carrie looked at her. "Well, I hope you know what you're doing."

"Carrie, when it comes to guys I always know what I'm doing," Sam replied smugly.

"Really?" Carrie asked. "Wasn't it you who fell for Johnny Angel. Twice?" She pushed the button for the electric window to go down so that cool salt air filled the car.

"This is not the same," Sam replied, taking a deep breath of ocean air and exhaling it slowly. "I told you, I like Danny as a friend. A friend."

38

"A friend," Carrie repeated. She took in Sam's ultrashort hot pink shift dress. "You wear that for friends?"

"Hey, Alden, gimme a break," Sam uttered. "I know you know what a guy friend is. Wasn't it you that almost married her guy friend, Raymond Saliverez, so he could get a green card and stay in the United States?"

"That was different," Carrie protested.

Sam sniffed and rolled her eyes, but in her heart knew that Carrie was right.

"How's he doing, anyway?" Sam asked, catching a glimpse on the horizon of the ferry as it approached.

"Raymond? Just fine."

"I liked him," Sam mused. "He was cute."

"Is there a guy alive you don't think is cute?" Carrie asked Sam as the ferry neared.

"Many," Sam replied solemnly. "Ian Templeton, for example."

"Ian Templeton is thirteen years old," Carrie said with mock exasperation as the ferry pulled into the dock.

"I rest my case," Sam retorted, as she and Carrie watched a horde of people coming down off the ferry.

"Just remember," Carrie said, "just because you think of Danny as 'only a friend' doesn't mean that that's how he thinks of you."

"Well, can I help it if I'm irresistible?" Sam asked, batting her eyes.

"Sam—" Carrie protested.

"I got the message, Car," Sam replied, scanning the crowd for Danny. "There he is!" She bounded from the car to meet her friend.

Danny came down off the ferry gangway and looked around uncertainly. He was wearing a plain white T-shirt, a pair of black Levi 505 jeans, and running shoes.

Wow, he looks hot! Sam thought. *He looks like he's gained a few pounds of muscle, and his hair has gotten longer, too.*

Unable to restrain herself, Sam started singing to get Danny's attention.

"M-I-C-K-E-Y M-O-U-S-E!"

Danny turned in the direction of her voice, spotted Sam, and walked rapidly over to her. Not bothering to put his small knapsack down, he embraced her. Sam let herself be enveloped in Danny's arms as they stood in the parking lot.

"I'm so happy to see you," Danny whispered to her.

"I'm glad to see you, too."

"I've missed you."

"Me too," Sam replied honestly.

"You are the world's worst letter writer," Danny murmured.

"I know," Sam replied.

Then Danny kissed Sam lightly on the lips, blushed, and let her go.

Hmm, still shy I see, Sam thought to herself. *But that's part of his appeal.*

"Carrie's here with me," Sam said, pointing to the Templetons' Mercedes. "Come on!"

"Nice car," Danny commented as they walked over to it. "She just win the lottery?"

"Belongs to the Templetons," Sam replied simply. "I'd trade employers with Carrie any day."

"You can always come back to Disney World," Danny joked, but there was wistfulness behind his voice.

"Hey, I got canned, remember?" Sam said.

"So, there's a new choreographer now!" Danny said.

"Hey, I'm on to bigger and better things," Sam said.

Carrie got out of the car as the two old friends approached, went over to Danny, and Danny embraced her as well.

"Great to see you again, Carrie," Danny said.

"You, too," Carrie replied, grinning at Danny.

"So what's the plan?" Danny asked.

"There's a party tonight at the Play Café on Main Street," Sam said, ushering Danny into the car. "I thought we'd stop by. You game?"

"You gonna be there?" Danny asked with a grin.

"Wouldn't miss it," Sam answered. "We get to see Carrie up on the silver screen."

"What are you talking about?" Danny

42

asked, sliding over to make room for his knapsack.

"We'll explain it on the way," Carrie said. "You are about to see the most humiliating moment of my life."

"Hey, I would give my right hooter to be in a movie," Sam said, "and here you are moaning about it!"

"Carrie was in a movie?" Danny asked as Carrie started the car. "No kidding?"

"No kidding," Sam replied, feeling all warm and happy just to have Danny there sitting behind her in the car. "And just think, it's been recorded for posterity! That means she can never, ever, ever live it down!"

During the drive to the Play Café, Sam told Danny the story of how Carrie had been picked to play the role of Luce Kittyn, a girl who gets slashed to death by the evil villain, in the slice-and-dice movie *Sunset Beach Slaughter,* which had been filmed on the island earlier in the summer. Now, someone had obtained the daily rushes of the slasher sequences of the movie, and

43

the sequences were going to be shown that evening on the Play Café's video monitors.

As Carrie's car pulled onto Main Street, Sam could see that word about the showing had spread quickly. There were dozens of cars parked outside the Café.

"This is going to be great!" Sam hooted. "There're tons of people here!"

"God, I hate this," Carrie said.

"I can pour some red paint on you for dramatic effect," Sam offered.

"Gee, you're a pal," Carrie replied dryly.

"Or maybe spray you with pig's blood or something," Sam continued. "Just so you'll feel more comfortable."

"I think it's cool," Danny said. "I'd love to be in a movie."

Sam led the way in. Usually, at this hour of evening, the Café was filled with kids hanging out, dancing, and gabbing, but tonight all the action was around the video monitors.

"You see Emma or Kurt anywhere?" Carrie asked Sam.

"Nope," Sam replied. "But someone who just came up on the video monitor looks suspiciously like you!" Sam pointed to a monitor that was just overhead.

Sam, Carrie, and Danny watched, in rapt fascination, as a scene from *Sunset Beach Slaughter* played out on the screen. They saw Carrie, dressed as Luce Kittyn, walking past the Play Café, which had been renamed the "Slay Café" for the movie. Then the pro wrestler Rocky Mountain, cast as the blade-wielding villain, grabbed Carrie and cut her throat with an enormous blade. Carrie screamed at the top of her lungs, as Rocky Mountain did his dastardly deed and bright-red blood ran down her white shirt.

When the scene was over, the crowd turned to where Sam, Carrie, and Danny were standing, and broke into wild applause, whooping, and hollering.

"Take a bow," Danny whispered to Carrie, poking her in the ribs.

"No way!" Carrie replied, holding her ground.

"Come on," Sam urged her, "this is your big moment."

"Great," Carrie groaned, but finally, because the cheering wouldn't stop, she stepped forward and kind of nodded her head.

Emma rushed over. She'd been trapped by the crowd under another of the monitors.

"Hey star," she said to Carrie, giving her a hug.

"I am so humiliated," Carrie said. "Seeing myself up there is not my idea of a good time."

"You have a number of screws loose, if you ask me," Sam told Carrie. "I mean, if you weren't my best friend I would be too jealous to allow you to live."

"It is exciting!" Emma agreed. "And you look great!"

"What I look is fat," Carrie said flatly. "I'm going to the ladies room." She walked away, Sam and Emma looking after her.

"Hey Emma," Danny said shyly, "it's good to see you again."

"Danny!" Emma cried, her voice full of warmth. "I'm glad to see you, too." Emma and Danny hugged. "Welcome to the island."

46

"Thanks," Danny replied with a grin.

"Kurt around?" Carrie asked Emma.

"He'll be here in a half-hour or so," Emma replied. "Just in time for the next show."

"Can you believe Carrie's reaction to this?" Sam asked, shaking her head. "She does not look fat!"

"I agree," Emma said, "but I bet it's disconcerting to see yourself on a big screen like that."

"It wouldn't be for me," Sam insisted. She turned to Danny. "So, you want to stay or you want to boogie?"

"How about a walk on the beach?" Danny suggested.

"Okay," Sam agreed. "Why don't we drop your stuff off at the Beach Youth Hostel— it's walking distance from here—and then we can go down to the ocean."

"That'd be great," Danny quickly agreed.

"Tell Carrie we left," Sam told Emma.

"Sure," Emma agreed.

"You think she's okay?"

"Carrie is about the most okay person I know," Emma said with a smile.

"Yeah, that's true," Sam agreed. She

47

turned to Danny. "Come on," she said, grabbing his hand. "We're outta here."

"Different from Orlando, huh?" Danny said to Sam, as they sat together on a big beach blanket on the main beach under the dark sky.

"Totally," Sam agreed. She listened to the waves breaking on the shore.

"Thanks for suggesting we leave the Café," Danny said. "I was feeling kind of uncomfortable in that zoo."

"My pleasure," Sam replied.

I really did want to get out of there because Danny felt uncomfortable, Sam thought to herself, *but I have to admit I also wanted to leave because I was afraid Pres might show up any minute! I thought I wouldn't care but once I got there, I did!*

"How are you going to get back home from here?" Danny asked her solicitously.

"Cab or trolley, no prob," Sam replied.

"Okay," Danny said. He sifted some sand between his fingers. They sat quietly for a moment.

"Tell me about your mother," Danny

48

finally said. "I got that postcard you sent me telling that you'd met her, but it was pretty cryptic."

"I'm not really in the mood," Sam replied. "Too serious."

"Okay, we'll talk about something else," Danny responded. "But I'm always here for you, to listen, when you're ready."

"Well, it's kind of like this," Sam began. And though she had absolutely no intention when she came to the beach of telling Danny the story of how she searched for, found, and then met her birth mother, Susan Briarly (Sam's adoptive parents had never even told her she was adopted—she'd found out earlier that summer by accident and still felt they had betrayed her), Sam found the story pouring out of her. It seemed easy to tell Danny everything.When she was done, she could feel tears threatening, but she willed them back.

"Wow," Danny breathed softly. "So, how do you feel now?"

"Like . . . like I don't actually have a mother, even though I have two," Sam said, amazed that she was able to put her feelings so clearly into words.

"Everyone needs a mother," Danny said gently. "It doesn't matter who you are."

Sam nodded agreement.

Danny looked at Sam, then shyly looked down at the sand. "You're so special, Sam, I know they both love you. How could they not? There's no one else in the whole world like you."

Sam laughed. "Is that good?"

"Sam," Danny said fervently, "that is great."

They lay back on their blanket, not touching, and looked up at the stars.

FOUR

"It's a *what* kind of contest?" Danny asked Sam.

"Belly-flop and Cannonball," Sam repeated. "Very big stuff with the country club set."

It was the next morning and Danny and Sam were standing near the main outdoor pool at the Sunset Country Club. Every summer since its founding, the club held a just-for-fun belly-flop/cannonball competition for any member or member's guest who cared to compete. Inside the snack bar were photographs of the annual winners going all the way back to 1948. The officers of the club were the official judges, and they sat, five men and women dressed in white, alongside the pool at a long table.

Sam had brought the Jacobs twins and Danny. Emma and Carrie were there, too, along with Ian Templeton, and Ethan and Wills Hewitt (whom Emma took care of).

"May I have your attention, ladies and gentlemen!" announced Kurt Ackerman—head swimming instructor at the club, and Emma's boyfriend—over the makeshift PA system. "First up in the annual Sunset Country Club International Invitational Belly-Flop and Cannonball Competition, hailing from Woodmere, Long Island—Howie Lawrence!"

Howie Lawrence, a thin, slightly nerdy-looking guy who was actually really nice, climbed to the top of the ten-foot-high dive, let out a Tarzan yell, and pounded his chest.

"OOOOOO-AAAAAH!"

The crowd of about two hundred people laughed and applauded.

"Howie Lawrence is so skinny he couldn't make a big enough splash to drown a flea," Sam snorted.

"Hey, aren't you the girl who was nick-named 'Stork' in high school because you were so thin?" Emma reminded Sam.

"I happen to be fashionably slender," Sam said regally.

"Howie looks cute," Carrie said, as Howie clowned around up on the diving board. "Besides, it's the spirit that counts. I don't see you getting up there."

"Is that a challenge?" Sam replied.

"Yup," Carrie smiled, winking at Danny.

"Accepted," Sam said emphatically, and then made her way over to the scorer's table to register.

"I'd better go with her," Danny grinned, "to keep her from bribing the judges."

As Sam and Danny walked to the table, Howie began his dive. He ran to the back of the board, took five quick steps to the end, bounced as high as he could and grabbed his knees.

SPLASH! He hit the water and it showered the spectators near him. The judges wrote on their pads, then held up Howie's scores. Mostly 5.5's and 5.6's on a scale of six.

"Not good enough to win," Sam sniffed. "I'll cream him."

"You'll have to cream me first," Danny laughed.

"You're entering?"

"Would I let you do this alone?" Danny countered.

"NEXT CONTESTANT!" Kurt's voice rang out again, drawing Sam and Danny's attention as they registered. "From Newburyport, Massachusetts, tipping the scales at 345 pounds, last year's winner, Big Mike Candleness!"

Sam and Danny watched in fascination as a short, unbelievably stocky man in a teeny-weenie bathing suit hidden somewhere under his stomach ascended the ladder to the springboard.

"He's the club golf champion," Sam murmured, "though I don't know how he even swings a club."

"You don't have to be skinny to play golf," Danny whispered back.

"Yeah, but you do have to be able to see the ball," Sam pointed out.

They stared up at the man on the diving board, who was now making muscle-man poses for the crowd.

"Last year he got straight sixes from the judges," Sam said. "After his belly-flop, they were putting on raincoats in Los Angeles."

They watched as Candleness took a running leap off the high board, went into a swan dive, but instead of entering the water headfirst, deliberately landed directly on his considerable belly.

A collective groan went up from the crowd, as water splashed everywhere. "Ouch!" Danny yelled, as Candleness made contact.

The judges held up their scorecards. Mostly 5.8's and 5.9's, though one judge gave Candleness a perfect score. Candleness emerged from the water like a victorious boxer, shaking his arms over his head, with his belly beet-red from the impact.

"Can't top that," Sam said. "I'm withdrawing."

"You're chickening out?" Danny asked.

"Call it a strategic retreat," Sam joked.

"Well, I'm still in," Danny said resolutely.

Sam's eyes widened with surprise. The Danny she knew would have been too shy

to do something like this—at least without his Goofy costume. Maybe he really
was getting more self-confident.

"Go for it," Sam retorted. "It's fun to finish second."

After a dozen more contestants, none of
whom came close to matching Candleness
for either style or form, Danny's name was
called. He stripped down to his swimsuit,
gave Sam a quick kiss on the cheek, and
headed off for the springboard.

Sam hurried back over to her friends
and started a chant.

"Goofy. Goofy! GOOFY! GOOFY!"

Soon, the entire crowd around the pool
was chanting "GOOFY!"—though most of
them had no idea what they chanting it
for.

Danny reached the top of the ladder.
He stretched and made a funny face at
the crowd, which only made them chant
louder. Then he stepped back, took a running start, and launched himself.

"Look at that!" Sam yelled.

Danny had launched into a double som-
ersault.

Just before he hit the water, he pulled himself into a supertight little ball. The splash from the water went up as far as the ten-foot-high diving board.

"Yes!" Sam exulted, as the crowd burst into applause. Danny climbed out of the pool with a huge grin on his face.

The crowd turned its attention to the judges, who seemed to be taking a long time to post their scores. After consulting with the others, one of the judges got up and went over to Kurt. Then she went back to the table and nodded her head. The rest of the judge's held up their scores.

"Ladies and gentlemen," Kurt's voice boomed out over the PA system, "we have a tie for first place. Will Danny Franklin and Mike Candleness please step forward to accept their awards."

Sam ran over to a dripping Danny and hugged him hard. "Go get 'em!" she cried, pushing him toward Kurt.

Danny shyly inched his way forward toward the judges' table.

"Where'd you learn to dive like that?" Sam yelled to him.

"Camp!" Danny replied.

"Why didn't you tell me you could dive?" Sam cried.

"You never asked," Danny answered, as he moved in next to Mike Candleness for his winner's photograph.

"And now for a really special treat, we have entertainment!" Lydia Grabel, president of the Sunset Country Club, trilled into the microphone.

Mondo-boring, Sam thought to herself, as she drummed her fingers on the table. Following the belly-flop contest they had all gone inside the country club for a buffet lunch. Sam had thought she'd be able to cut out, but now it appeared that she had to sit through something called "entertainment."

"Probably a string quartet that'll put us all to sleep," Sam muttered to Danny.

"Wrong, like always," Becky Jacobs sang out. "I know what it is and you don't!"

"For the entertainment portion of our post-competition lunch, we are proud to present a special dance exhibition by

58

Christopher McGriff, artistic director of the Long Beach Bay Ballet Company, a special guest of our very own Mr. and Mrs. Bill Peters!" Lydia announced.

X! I haven't thought about him for at least . . . a day! Sam realized. *So now I'll see if he's really such a great dancer after all.*

As the crowd applauded, Sam leaned over to Danny. "I heard this guy is really good," she whispered.

"He is," Allie insisted, having overheard Sam. "Maybe he could teach you a thing or two."

"Sam's a great dancer," Danny told Allie. "She was the best dancer at Disney World."

Allie gave Danny a bored look. "Why should I believe a guy who dresses in a Goofy costume?"

Before Danny could reply, hot tango music came over the sound system.

X glided into the room dressed in a Spanish toreador's outfit. He strutted over to the club president at the head table—she had to be at least seventy years old—

and extended his hand in an invitation that she couldn't refuse. She looked thrilled, in fact, as X led her onto the dance floor.

"Wow, he's great!" Sam exclaimed, as X started to lead the woman around in a hot tango.

"He's good," Carrie agreed.

"Really good," Emma seconded.

"I want to have his children," Allie Jacobs added.

"Shut up," Sam retorted.

A minute or so later, with the older woman totally out of breath, the tango ended, and the room burst again into applause. When the clapping ended, another song came up on the sound system—Elvis Presley's version of "Jailhouse Rock." X stripped off his black hat and silk shirt—his hair was slicked back, greaser-style, and he had on a plain black T-shirt. Instantly, he'd transformed himself into a '50s greaser. Then, he looked around for someone to dance with.

Oh my God, Sam realized. *He's coming right this way. He's coming right to our table.*

"Me! Me!" Allie and Becky Jacobs clamored simultaneously. "You want me!"

But X just smiled his beguiling smile and ignored them.

Oh my God. He's coming right at me.

X stopped in front of Sam and extended his hand. Sam reached out and took it. They took the floor and began an energetic jitterbug. As soon as X realized how good Sam was, he added more complex spins, leaps, and throws. Sam kept up with him every step of the way.

I'm flying. I swear I'm flying! Sam thought giddily.

She wanted to go further and further, and he led her into even more complex moves. Then, at the very end, he lifted Sam off the ground and spun her over his head. The number ended with X's arms fully extended, Sam eight feet off the ground, and her wild red hair spilling like a waterfall toward the floor.

The place went totally wild.

This is what I'm meant to do! Sam realized, her heart pounding with adrenaline. *And this is the guy I'm meant to do it with!*

X brought Sam back down to earth and to her feet.

"Hey, you're a ringer," he said, grinning at her.

"I'm a professional," Sam said, "if that's what you mean. I tried to tell you that at the beach the other day."

X looked puzzled.

"You were with Diana and Lorell?" Sam reminded him.

"Oh, yeah, that's right!" X said, snapping his fingers. "You're Sandi?"

"Sam," Sam corrected him. "Listen, it was great dancing with you."

"Mutual," X said. "I'd say the crowd loved us." He kissed Sam lightly on the cheek, and held up her arm like she was a professional boxer.

The place went wild again. Sam and X bowed to the cheering crowd.

This is what I'm meant to do, Sam thought again. *And this is the guy I'm meant to do it with.*

FIVE

"Sam, no lie, you were awesome this afternoon," Becky Jacobs said, taking another sip of her Coke.

"Totally," chimed in Allie, staring at Sam, wide-eyed.

"You should have seen her, Dad," Becky continued to her father, who had just sat down at the dining room table. "She dances like one of those girls on MTV!"

Sam grinned at Danny and at Ian Templeton, who were both at dinner with the Jacobses. Danny was her guest, and Ian had been invited by Becky. Becky and Allie were backup singers for Ian's band, Lord Whitehead and the Zit People. Ian had long had a crush on Becky, but Becky only liked older guys and usually didn't give Ian the time of day.

"It's not a date," Becky had told Sam earlier.

"So what is it?" Sam had joked with her.

"It's dinner," Becky had insisted. "How can it be a date? My father's going to be there."

"So, what is this new interest in Ian?" Sam had asked Becky.

"Ian is an artist," Becky had said, as if Sam was too dumb to live.

As soon as dinner was served, the twins proceeded to give their dad and Ian a blow-by-blow description of the day's events, including the belly-flop competition and Sam and X's dance exhibition.

"I told you she was the best dancer at Disney World," Danny reminded them, cracking into one of the fresh Maine lobsters they'd prepared.

"Yeah, you did," Becky admitted. "And you're a great diver," Becky added. "Did you dive at Disney World, too?"

"'Fraid not," Danny answered, spearing a piece of lobster with his fork. "Except to get away from six-year-olds whose idea of a good time was to try to play king of the hill on my costume!"

"I think it's so cool when a guy is talented," Becky murmured, looking right at Ian Templeton. Ian caught Becky's glance and blushed a deep shade of red.

Uh oh, Sam thought. *I see one order of young love coming up, hold the pickles, hold the onions. Imagine Becky Jacobs finally returning the long-unanswered love call of Ian Templeton!*

"We . . . we . . . well," Ian stammered finally, "I think it's so cool when, like, a girl is really talented, and all the guys in the band think that you and Allie really add a lot to our sound."

Allie turned to Danny. "You see, Ian has a band called Lord Whitehead and the Zit People—we play industrial music—and me and Becky are the backup singers."

"So I've heard," Danny smiled. Sam had told him the story of Ian's band, whose music consisted mostly of banging on the insides of old washing machines, clothes dryers, and other home appliances with sticks and pipes, while singing along to recorded cassettes of rock classics.

"Aren't you girls going to eat?" Dan Jacobs asked his daughters.

"Dad!" Becky scolded him. "We're discussing something serious here."

"Ah, yes," Mr. Jacobs responded in a patronizing tone. "Great art."

"Well, you don't get it because you're old," Allie told her father. "Even Sam is too old to appreciate what's really cutting edge."

"I'm too old?" Sam asked.

"Sam," Becky said with exaggerated patience. "You're *nineteen*!"

"Yeah, like you don't wish you were," Sam shot back. She caught a glimpse of Mr. Jacobs's frown out of the corner of her eye, and realized she should take a more "mature" tack with the twins. She changed the subject. "So . . . how do you like the lobster, Danny?" she asked.

"I think it's great," Danny said, "but I've only had it a couple of times in my life."

"You allergic?" Ian Templeton asked, taking his nutcracker and cracking open one of the claws.

"Not exactly," Danny replied. "I grew up in a kosher home."

"What's that?" Ian asked him, puzzled.

"I know!" Becky clamored to explain.

"Yeah," Allie chimed in, "we learned it in Hebrew school—"

"—which was sooooo boring," Becky said, looking directly at her dad.

"—but we had to do it to study for our bat mitzvahs last year," Allie finished.

"Why don't one of you explain to Ian what kosher is?" Mr. Jacobs suggested, a slightly exasperated tone in his voice.

I'd like to know too, Sam thought.

"Well," Becky started out, "in pretty religious Jewish families—"

"—they follow a lot of rules about what you can eat—" Allie chimed in.

"—like for example you can't eat pork, or drink milk with a meat dish—"

"—or eat stuff like shrimp and clams and lobster, right Danny?" Allie asked.

Danny nodded. "That's pretty much on target. It's called keeping kosher. And my family kept kosher for a long time."

Whoa baby, Sam thought. *Danny Franklin is Jewish? And kosher? Wow. We never even talked about it. Did I tell him that*

67

*my birth father was Israeli and my birth
mother's mother is Jewish? I think so. Well,
I know I wrote him something about it on a
postcard. Wait, how could I have gotten all
that on a postcard . . .*

"So, what's the point?" Ian asked Danny,
interrupting Sam's train of thought. "Why
don't people just eat what they want?"

"No one really knows the exact reason,"
Danny admitted. "The rules are in the Old
Testament."

"My teacher said that it's because thousands of years ago the stuff you couldn't
eat could be bad for you," Allie suggested.

"That's what some people think," Danny
agreed. "But I was always taught that the
main reason is so you don't just take for
granted the food that you eat."

"Why'd you stop?" Ian asked.

"It was a personal decision," Danny said,
matter-of-factly. "If you're interested, Ian,
we can talk about it later."

*Whoa baby. Danny Franklin is Jewish.
I've got a lot of questions for him that I've
been wondering about. A whole lot of questions.*

Sam flopped down on her bed and looked at the clock—nearly midnight. With a yawn, she picked up the book that Danny had bought for her at the Sunset Island Booksmith right after dinner.

It was a novel called *The Chosen*, written by a guy with a weird name, Chaim Potok, which Danny had told her was a Hebrew name.

"My birth mother, Susan, taught me a toast in Hebrew," Sam had told Danny in the bookstore, after he picked out the book for her. "It goes, 'L'Chaim!' It means 'to life!'"

"That's what this guy's first name means," Danny had replied. "Life."

"Cool," Sam had replied.

Immediately after dinner with the Jacobs family, Sam had tried to question Danny about Judaism, but he had merely grinned and said that he wanted Sam to read a book first.

So he got me to drive us to the bookstore. I figured for sure he was going to buy me some boring textbook or a question and answer book. And instead he gets me a novel by some guy named Life. Weird.

But Sam was game—even though she usually hated to read. After she dropped Danny off at the hostel, she went home and started the novel. So far, she had read about thirty pages, and she loved it—the book was set during the 1940s and started off with a baseball game between two teams of Jewish teenagers, one of them super-religious.

Can you believe it? I'm actually, voluntarily, on my own, no teacher telling me, just because I want to, reading a book? But it's been an amazing day.

She laid back on her bed and stared at the ceiling. Danny was so special, maybe the most special guy she'd ever known. Then an image of X swam into her head—the two of them dancing together as if they were made for each other. And then another image invaded her mind—sloe-eyed, long and lean, the hottest guy on two feet—Pres. Since she'd left her message on his answering machine, she still hadn't heard from him.

Well, Danny's scheduled to leave tomor-row night, so Pres can't be too upset, Sam thought sleepily. *I may have pulled all of this off to perfection. God, I'm good.*

But what about X?

Sam fell asleep with the book open on her chest, and that question firmly on her mind.

"I can't believe we both got the day off!" Carrie called to Sam over the loud music pulsing out of the sound system in the car. Carrie was driving, Billy sat next to her, and Sam and Danny were in the back seat. Carrie headed the car south on Route 1 toward Kennebunkport, Wells, and Ogunquit.

"Hey, Mr. Jacobs has a heart," Sam quipped. "Not a very big one, but it beats. Anyway, he likes Danny a lot. Can you blame him?"

Billy leaned over to turn down the music, then turned around to face Sam. "I heard the tapes from our session the other night."

Uh oh, Sam thought nervously. *Was I awful?*

"So?" she asked noncommittally.

"They were pretty good," Billy responded.

Relief flooded through Sam. *At least he didn't say they were awful—meaning that I was awful,* Sam thought to herself.

"What did Pres think of it?" Sam asked.

"Hasn't heard 'em yet," Billy responded. "He and Sly went smallmouth bass fishing up in the Belgrade Lakes. They'll be back tomorrow night."

"Oh, that's cool," Sam said nonchalantly. She looked over at Danny, who didn't seem to pick up on the fact that they were discussing Sam's boyfriend.

"It's pretty good up there," Danny commented. "I went to summer camp near China."

"China?" Carrie asked, keeping her eye on the road.

"China, Maine," Danny responded. "Up near Waterville."

"Weird name for a town," Carrie said.

"There's also a Paris, Naples, and Norway in this state," Danny commented.

"Major metropolitan centers, huh?" Sam joked, as she settled back and looked out the window. They were making steady progress down the coast, and had just passed through Old Orchard Beach—a town with a slightly hokey amusement-park atmosphere and filled with cars with license plates from Quebec, Canada.

In another forty-five minutes, they were at the quaint town of Ogunquit. Carrie parked in the large parking lot near the beach, and together they took a walk along something called the Marginal Way—a footpath that wound along rocky cliffs and went on for a mile or more. From time to time, Carrie stopped them to take photographs of the crashing surf and the exquisite rock formations. Carrie and Billy walked ahead, hand in hand, while Sam and Danny followed behind.

At the end of the path were a bunch of shops, and they all went into a place called Barnacle Billy's to eat. They placed their order at one window, found a table in the open air overlooking Ogunquit's small lobster-boat harbor, and it wasn't long before a waitress brought them two huge platters of steamed clams, steamed mussels, corn on the cob, and iced tea.

"Ah," Sam said, kicking back, "this is the life."

"You said it," Carrie agreed, digging into the steamers.

"I started reading a book Danny gave me last night," Sam announced to Carrie and Billy. "It's really good."

Billy looked at her sideways.

"Could you repeat that?" he asked, grinning.

"A book, Billy," Sam smiled. "Pages with words on them. In English. Surely you've heard of them."

"Yeah," Billy replied, "I just remember your saying that you hate to read, that you never read, etcetera, etcetera. This guy is a great influence on you."

"So, what are you reading?" Carrie asked.

"*The Chosen*," Sam replied with dignity. "A novel. I'll lend it to you when I'm done."

When they'd finished off the food, they started back on the Marginal Way toward the main beach at Ogunquit. They were planning to climb up on the dunes there and watch the sun set over the tidal pools just west of the beach. As before, Billy and Carrie walked ahead, and Sam and Danny trailed behind.

"They couldn't believe I'm reading a book," Sam said to Danny as they walked.

"I can believe it," Danny answered.

"They think . . . well some people think I'm not too intellectual," Sam said honestly. "Actually, *everyone* thinks that!"

"Who's everyone?" Danny asked, picking up a smooth stone and tossing it high into the air.

"My teachers back in Kansas, my sister, my friends," Sam enumerated.

"What about your mother and father in Kansas?" Danny asked her, as they rounded a particularly spectacular vista.

Sam reflected for a moment. "They never said I was stupid," she said finally, "but they never really gave me a lot of encouragement, either. My little sister, Ruth Ann, was always the smart one."

They walked in silence for a few minutes.

"Well," Danny finally said, "here's what I think. I think you're the whole package. Gorgeous. Talented. Nice. And very, very smart."

Sam felt a wave of warmth roll through her. No one had ever said anything like that to her before. Most guys never got beyond the first item that Danny had listed.

Sam turned to look at Danny. "Really? You think I'm smart?"

Danny nodded. "I know so."

She smiled at him. "You're the greatest, Danny Franklin," she said, giving him a warm hug.

Danny hugged her back. Suddenly, Sam felt heat between them, and the hug didn't seem so innocent anymore. But when she pulled away there was only Danny's sweet, trusting, gorgeous face.

"Hey, you never told me you're Jewish," Sam said as they started walking again. "Why didn't you tell me?"

"Would it have mattered?" Danny asked.

Sam laughed. "You're not gonna believe what I found out about my birth family. . . ." She proceeded to tell him all about being part Jewish by birth. "It's very weird," she concluded. "I mean, back in Junction, Kansas, I think there were maybe two Jewish families or something."

"So that's why you were suddenly so interested in learning about Judaism!" Danny said with a chuckle. "See, that's what I mean, Sam, about your being smart. You have a really inquiring mind—this is just an example."

"Yeah, I kind of do, don't I?" Sam agreed happily.

"Absolutely," Danny said firmly. He reached for Sam's hand and squeezed it warmly.

Without giving it a thought, Sam squeezed back, then she kept his hand in hers, and they followed Carrie and Billy along the path, hand in hand.

SIX

By the time Sam, Danny, Carrie, and Billy got back to the island late that evening, Danny had already called his friend Kenny and postponed his departure until the following afternoon. Although she noticed the strange looks from Carrie and Billy in the front seat, Sam thought she'd never been so comfortable as she fell asleep on the ride home with her head on Danny's shoulder and his arm around her.

Once on the island, Carrie dropped Sam at the Jacobs's. Sam tiptoed into the dimly lit kitchen, expecting everyone to be asleep.

"Hiya!" a voice called to her.

"Becky," Sam whispered, "it's almost midnight. What are you doing up?"

"Writing," Becky responded, from her

seat at the kitchen table. "Have a fun day?"

What's this? Becky Jacobs being civil to me? There must be something wrong.

"Pretty good," Sam answered, sitting down near Becky.

"I like Danny," Becky said, barely picking her head up from whatever she was writing.

"I like him too," Sam agreed, picking at some grapes that were in a fruit bowl next to Becky.

A lot, she admitted to herself. *Especially after today.*

"What're you writing?" Sam continued.

"Oh, nothing important," Becky responded, as nonchalantly as she could. "Just some poetry."

"Poetry," Sam repeated. She could not have been more surprised if Becky had reported that she was translating the Declaration of Independence into Arabic.

"Yeah," Becky mumbled, still looking at the paper instead of looking at Sam. "Poetry."

"Oh," Sam said, reaching for more grapes. "What's it about?"

"It's private."

"Can I read it sometime?"

"Maybe," Becky answered.

"Only if you want me to," Sam assured her.

"There's a message for you from Pres on the answering machine," Becky said without looking up from her writing. "He called this afternoon from someplace called North Belgrade."

Sam felt the red color that was rising slowly in her cheeks.

"He's up there fishing," she said to Becky, though she had no idea at all why she felt she had to justify herself to Becky Jacobs.

"Oh," Becky answered. "Anyway, I know it's none of my business, but I think Danny is a really cool guy and would be a good boyfriend for you. Better than Pres."

"How come?" Sam asked before she could stop herself.

Becky shrugged. "Danny is deeper. Like Ian."

"Like Ian," Sam repeated, fighting the urge to laugh.

"Yeah," Becky replied. She looked over

at Sam. "Don't you think Ian is a way-cool name?"

"Sure," Sam said, trying to take in this bizarre conversation. What was going on here? Becky had always had a crush on Pres. Becky thought Ian was too young and sort of dweeby. And Becky did not write poetry in the middle of the night.

"What rhymes with Ian?" Becky mused, her pen in her mouth. "Bein'? Seein'?"

"I'll just go check Pres's message," Sam said, not sure how to reply.

"I like believin," Becky decided, and bent back over her writing.

Weird. Extremely weird, Sam thought to herself as she padded as quietly as she could into the family room where the answering machine was located. She ran the tape back to the beginning, and pressed the Play button.

"Hey Sam," Presley Travis said from the machine, his voice even more neutral and laconic than usual, "Sly and I are up here in the Belgrades doing some fishing. I understand you have a friend visitin' you. Wish you'd a told me when I saw you last. You and I need to have a talk when I get back. That'll be in a day or two. Or maybe three. Who knows?"

That was it. The electronic marker on the tape said the message was left at 4:20 that afternoon.

Sam shrugged. *That wasn't so bad,* she thought to herself. *He could have been a lot more angry. He's been more irritated with me than that before. Looks like I pulled off a Sam-gets-every-guy-she-wants play once again!*

But somehow, this time, the thought didn't make her happy. Instead of getting that rush-feeling somewhere in her stomach, that confident I-am-the-baddest feeling, she felt depressed. Sad. Anxious. Kind of awful.

This isn't fun anymore, she realized, sitting down in the chair next to the answering machine. *I'm caught between two guys, both of whom I really like a lot. Why is it that I can never make up my mind, never commit to anyone? Why is it that I want everyone to love me, but I can't seem to really love anyone back?*

She trudged up the stairs and went to bed without any answers.

Sam and Danny sat together on a bench overlooking the Sunset Island ferryport. Danny was scheduled to catch the three o'clock afternoon ferry back to the mainland in fifteen minutes. Then, he was going to catch a bus in Portland that would get him to Ellsworth to meet his friend Kenny five hours later.

"A lot of traveling in a little time," he told Sam, holding her hand in his as he talked, "but you're worth it."

"Thanks," Sam replied gratefully. "I'm glad you stayed the extra day, and I'm glad that you're my friend."

"You know, Sam," Danny said, looking out at the water as he spoke, "I've always wanted to be more than just your friend."

Sam was quiet for a minute before she spoke. That familiar uncomfortable feeling she felt whenever a guy started talking to her about being serious began to well up in the pit of her stomach.

I wish it'd go away, she cried to herself. *Please go away*. But, still, the feeling was there.

"I'm going to miss you," Danny said fervently.

"I'll miss you, too," Sam replied. "Hey, you're the first guy that's gotten me to read a novel in years!" she added, trying to inject some levity into the conversation.

"Did you finish reading *The Chosen*?" Danny asked her.

Sam nodded. "Just last night. I couldn't sleep and I read until past three. It was a great book." She looked over at Danny. "It was about . . . finding your place in this world, right? Trying to figure out where you belong?"

"Yeah," Danny agreed, smiling at Sam. "And who you belong with." He turned Sam's hand over in his. "I think . . . well, I think we belong together."

Sam gulped hard. "You do?"

Danny nodded. "I know you, Sam," he said fervently. "Better than any guy has ever known you. Maybe better than anyone," Danny continued. "You told me that yourself."

"Yeah," Sam said softly.

"And I know how difficult all this is for you," Danny said. "Love, and everything, you know."

"Yeah," she squeaked out again.

They were silent for nearly ten minutes, sitting together, waiting for the ferry. It finally pulled into the ferryport, and passengers started loading and unloading.

"I've got to go," Danny said finally.

Why can't I tell him what I really think, what I really want, how torn up inside I am? Sam thought to herself. She tried to make her mouth move and say the words, but nothing happened, no matter what she told her lips to do.

"There's no one like you, Danny," Sam finally said, even though it was a tiny fraction of what she wanted to say.

Danny looked at her with a slightly cock-eyed expression on his face. "To know me is to love me," he said, using one of Sam's favorite sayings. Then he bent over and kissed Sam gently on the lips. She kissed him back. They clung together on the bench, as the ferryboat captain blew the whistle, warning everyone the boat was about to depart.

Danny stood up, bent over and kissed Sam one more time, and was gone.

Sam stared at the clock—eight p.m.— and then down at the blank sheet of notebook paper on the small desk that she ordinarily used as a vanity. All of her cosmetics were crowded over into a corner to make room for her notebook. A lipstick fell over on to the paper and she shoved it into a drawer haphazardly.

She'd felt so out of it since Danny had left that afternoon that she intended to write him a letter. But now that she actually had paper and pen out, she had no idea what to say.

So she stared at the empty paper. Finally, she reached down, picked up the red felt-tip pen she'd found in her pocketbook, and started to write.

Dear Danny,
I'm not much of a letter writer, as you know. I just wanted you to know how

grateful I am that you came to visit me here on the island. It meant a lot to me, and I think we got to know each other a lot better. Do you think I'm difficult? I do! You are so good to me, so good for me, and I don't even give you the love you deserve, even though I want to. If I sound like I'm confused it's because I am. But you are such a friend that I am not afraid to tell you. That's weird, isn't it?

I want you to come back again soon. And stay longer next time.

Sam drew a heart, and wrote her name in the middle of it. Then she stopped and reread what she had written.

It isn't exactly what I mean to say, she thought, *but I'm not sure what it is I mean to say. Do I care so much for Danny now because he's gone, and it's safe for me to feel this way? And what about Pres? Where does he fit in to all of this?*

Sam checked the time again. She was shocked to see it was ten o'clock—she was supposed to pick Becky and Allie up at the country club at ten thirty, at a special juniors dance class with X.

How could I have spent so much time writing so little? she thought forlornly. *When are things going to start to be easy for me, for a change, instead of always being such a struggle?*

"So, listen to this," Becky told Sam as Sam drove the twins back from the country club. "Ian knows everything about rock and roll. Ian says the last really great rock band was The Who!"

"Yeah, as in 'who cares'?" Allie put in with disdain.

"Well, you should, if you call yourself a musician," Becky shot back to her sister.

"Get a grip, Becky," Allie groaned. "Everything Ian Templeton says is not brilliant."

"More brilliant than you," Becky shot back.

"Becky's in love with a child, Becky's in love with a child," Allie singsonged.

Sam rolled her eyes and tried to pay attention to her driving. She wasn't planning on having the ride back from the country club turn into major warfare.

"Why don't you guys tell me about the dance class?" Sam suggested, hoping to change the subject.

"X is the coolest," Allie said quickly. "I think he really likes me. He said I had a lot of talent."

"He did not," Becky corrected her sister. "He told Tasha Adams she had talent, not you."

Becky rolled her eyes and looked over at Sam. "Allie's just pissed because she's too young for X."

"Am not," Allie snapped. "You're the one going out with someone a year younger than you."

"Eight months," Becky defended herself. "Ian is eight months younger."

"Oh, Ian," Allie crooned in a high, goofy voiced imitation of her sister, "you're so cute and little and such a baby, but I just love you anyway, you stud-puppet!"

"Shut up!" Becky yelled, reaching across the seat to swat at her sister.

"Make me!" Allie yelled back.

"Chill out, you two, or you are in serious trouble," Sam said in her best no-nonsense voice. "What steps did X teach you?" she asked, trying to steer the conversation back to neutral ground.

"A line dance," Allie replied, still shooting hateful looks at her sister. "It was fun."

"Too country." Becky frowned. "Ugh."

"All good music doesn't have to be industrial music," Allie maintained.

"Well, Ian says—" Becky began.

"I don't care what Ian says!" Allie exclaimed.

"Then you don't have to be in the Zit People," Becky said haughtily.

Sam turned on the radio as loud as it would go to drown out the twins for the last few minutes of their trip home. When they got there, Allie ran off ahead of them into the house.

"Allie is just ticked off because she doesn't know what love is," Becky said to Sam, as she was getting out of the car.

"Neither do I," Sam said back, locking the car doors behind her. "Neither do I."

When she finally got inside the Jacobs

house, Sam saw that the phone answering machine light was blinking again. She reached over automatically and pressed the Play button. Pres's Tennessee drawl came over the machine again.

"Hey Sam," he said, "Me and Sly came back tonight. And I sure would like to talk to you. In fact, you might say we need to talk. So how about you call me when you get back in, no matter how late? You got the number."

Pres's voice clicked off. It was the only message on the machine.

Sam knew that she had to call him back. Now.

She went to the bottom of the stairs and listened for the twins, who seemed to be quiet for the moment.

Okay, she thought to herself, that bad feeling forming again in the pit of her stomach. *Here goes nothing.*

She dialed the Flirts' phone number, her heart pounding, not at all prepared for what she might be about to face.

SEVEN

Pres's familiar voice answered the phone.

"Hey," Sam heard him say, "Pres speakin'."

Sam's stomach formed that all-too-familiar knot.

"Hi," she said hesitantly, "it's me, Sam."

"Glad I could get you to return a phone call," Pres said easily.

Sam bit her lip nervously and switched the phone to her other ear. "So . . . how was your fishing trip?"

"Okay," Pres responded, his voice neutral. "How was your friend's visit?"

"Okay," Sam replied cautiously.

"He's that guy you met in Florida, right?" Pres asked.

"Right."

"That you like only as a friend," Pres continued.

"Right," Sam said again, hoping that there was an easy way out of this.

"Uh-huh," Pres said. "Well, it seems pretty strange that if some guy who you like 'only as a friend' comes to visit you, you'd do everything you can to avoid having the two of us meet up."

"Well, I guess I didn't know you'd want to meet him," Sam replied. *Yeah, that even sounds dumb to me,* she told herself.

"So, what did you tell him about me?" Pres asked her.

"Uh, not much," Sam admitted.

"Why not?"

"He didn't ask," Sam answered honestly, though she felt as if she was actually telling a lie.

Silence.

"You know," Pres said finally, "it's late, and I'm gettin' a mite tired."

"Me too," Sam chimed in, "I haven't slept—"

"That's not what I'm tired of," Pres interrupted her. "I'm tired of being played like a fiddle, if you catch my drift. Second fiddle."

"But I don't—" Sam protested.

"Sure you do," Pres interrupted her again. "You hide and you hide and you go behind my back, and you think good ol' Pres'll always understand."

"But he's just a friend," Sam tried to defend herself.

"Sam," Pres said finally, and Sam got the sense that he was trying to calm himself down. "You and I talked after the tour, when you had that thing with Johnny Angel, right?"

"Yeah," Sam said softly.

"And I agreed with you when you called it temporary insanity, didn't I?" Pres asked.

"That's what it was!" Sam exclaimed. "This is nothing like that!"

"Well, you were entitled to a little temporary insanity," Pres said. "But like you said, this ain't nothing like that."

"Pres, Danny is just a friend," Sam said in a low voice.

"Sam, you're probably right. He may be just a friend," Pres replied, his voice sounding as if it were coming between gritted teeth. "But I'm gonna tell you just one more time—I don't play second fiddle."

"I'm not playing around with you!" Sam answered, and this time, she really felt it in her heart.

"Don't take advantage of me," Pres warned. "I don't like it."

"I won't, I'm not—"

"Because what I said after the tour was also true," Pres continued. "If you're ready for more of a commitment, I'm ready, too. I thought we agreed on that."

"We did," Sam acknowledged, feeling sick to her stomach.

Oh, not tonight, Sam said to herself. *Let's not get into this tonight. I'm just too mixed up.*

"Let's talk about this more when we see each other, okay?" Sam finally suggested.

"Okay," Pres said. "But you better give this serious thought, Sam."

"I will," she promised. "I really will. Can we see each other tomorrow?" Sam asked.

"Uh-uh—I have to go to Boston to buy some stuff for the band. How about the day after?" Pres suggested.

"You got it," Sam said.

Sam finally hung up the phone, feeling as if she had dodged a bullet.

"So many guys, so little time," Sam sang out with her usual bravado, as she put her feet up on the deck of the outdoor café overlooking the first tee of the Sunset Country Club. She had just finished telling Carrie and Emma about her conversation with Pres.

It was the next evening, and when their chores were done, the girls had met up as they had planned earlier that day. But instead of going to the Play Café, Emma suggested that they dress up and go listen to a jazz trio at the country club. Kurt planned to join them around ten o'clock.

"Hey, remember when they had a rule that we couldn't be at the country club unless we were here with someone from the family we worked for?" Sam recalled. "Boy, that rule really ticked me off."

"I'm glad they changed it," Emma said.

"Oh, they would have made an exception

for you, anyway," Sam replied. "After all, you could buy the entire country club."

"Hey, ragging on Emma about her money is only your way of changing the subject," Carrie pointed out. "We want to know what you told Pres."

"I told him we'd talk about it more tomorrow when I see him," Sam replied with a sigh. She stared out at the golf course. "I don't see why we have to get all complicated about this."

"You're not being fair," Emma said softly. "When you got hurt on tour, Pres realized that he loves you, remember? Love is supposed to be a gift!"

"Hey, look who's talking!" Sam protested. "You're in love with Kurt, but you sure lost it for my brother Adam, when we were in California! I thought the West Coast was going to erupt in flames!"

"We were talking about you, not me," Emma replied, blushing.

"Oh, let's not talk about guys," Sam said, jumping up. "What do you think of the uni?" She spun around, showing off the full-skirted white chiffon cocktail dress she'd borrowed from Emma. On Emma it came to just above the knee; on Sam it was extremely short. She'd tied a piece of black velvet around her neck, choker-fashion, and finished the outfit with high, black velvet shoes that she'd found at a used-clothes shop.

"Elegant," Carrie replied. "If it wasn't for the fact that that skirt barely covers your panties, I'd hardly know it was you."

"Well, I can't disappoint my public," Sam said, sitting again. "You guys look great, too."

Carrie had on a black catsuit with a black mesh sweater over it, and Emma had on a simple pink silk shift that she'd bought in Paris.

"So glad you approve," Emma said. "Now let's talk about Pres and Danny."

"Pushy, pushy, pushy," Sam sang.

Emma poured herself another glass of iced tea from the pitcher on the table. "Sam, can you be serious for once?"

"Hey, I don't recall committing any crimes, here. Can I help it if half the male population falls for my charms?"

"No," Carrie said slowly, "but—"

"But nothing," Sam cut in. "Last time I looked, I'm not married—not even engaged. Or even engaged to be engaged."

"Don't you care about Pres?" Emma asked her.

"Sure," Sam replied, taking a big gulp of iced tea. "Who wouldn't?"

"So what are you doing leading Danny on?" Carrie asked her. "I mean, Billy Sampson has eyes. I'm sure he told Pres everything."

"That Danny is one of my best friends?" Sam scoffed. "That I put my head on his shoulder for the ride home? That he really cares about me a lot?"

"Sam," Emma tried again, "I think—"

"Please," Sam shrugged her off. "We are three fine babes not even twenty years old. Isn't this getting a little heavy?"

Carrie and Emma looked at each other.

Once again Sam got that terrible knot in her stomach. *It isn't working the way it used to,* she realized anxiously. *I'm not convincing myself. I can't just keep doing this!*

"I just don't want to see anyone get hurt," Emma finally said.

"One of these days you might have to grow up, Sam," Carrie added.

"Gee, no one told me it was lecture-Sam-night," Sam said lightly.

"Sam—" Carrie began.

"Okay, I heard you both, honest," Sam said sincerely. "I don't want anyone to get hurt, either. I'm . . . I'm confused. I admit it."

"Well, that's a start," Emma said.

"It's gonna have to do for the moment," Sam replied, lifting her heavy red hair from her neck. "Hey, isn't it about time for the music to start?"

All the people out on the veranda started drifting into the main ballroom, where the entertainment was to take place.

"I can't believe I actually talked the two of you into doing this," Emma marveled.

"Hey," Sam said, "I'll try anything once."

"That's the problem," Carrie said. But this time she said it with a smile on her face, and the three friends laughed as they went into the ballroom.

101

*　　*　　*

A tuxedoed headwaiter led the three girls to a small table just off the dance floor.

"Quel chic," Sam opined. "I need to mix with the rich and snooty more often."

"Would you ladies care to order a drink?" the waiter asked them politely.

"Diet Coke, please," Carrie said.

"Another iced tea, please," Emma requested.

"Do you have milk shakes?" Sam asked innocently.

"No, I'm sorry, we don't," the waiter answered, a smile twitching the corners of his mouth. "Would you like something else?"

"A Coke, then," Sam decided. "Do you have food?"

"Various hors d'oeuvres," the waiter said.

"Oh, bring a variety of that," Sam said airily. "A large variety, please."

"Certainly," the waiter agreed and walked away.

"Medical science should study you," Carrie marveled.

"What, I only had four pieces of fried chicken, some fries, some salad and two pieces of pie for dinner," Sam recalled. "I'm starved!"

"I hope you guys like the music," Emma said, looking over at the musicians as they tuned up.

"Like I said, I'll try anything once," Sam reminded her, "though I'm not crazed for jazz."

"Josh loves John Coltrane," Carrie mused fondly, remembering that her ex-boyfriend Josh, whom she had gone out with all through high school, was a big jazz fan.

"Do you ever miss him?" Emma asked Carrie.

"Sometimes," Carrie admitted. "But at least I did the honest thing." She gave Sam a pointed look.

"Aren't we subtle," Sam mumbled.

For a time, the girls sat quietly, listening to the five-piece Tommy Parsons Quintet play a couple of fast-paced numbers. Then, the quintet switched its focus toward old standards. Sam recognized the song "Sentimental Journey." A number of couples made their way out onto the dance floor.

"Care to dance?" a male voice said to Sam. "Sandi, isn't it?"

Sam turned to face the voice.

It was X.

He looked great.

Better than great, Sam thought, giving him the quick once-over. X wore a black Italian-style tuxedo with red butter-leather shoes. *It might look ridiculous on anyone else, but whoa baby, not on him!*

"No, it isn't, and yes, I would," Sam said, rising dramatically to her feet after taking the hand that X had extended to her.

X grinned. "Sorry Sam," he said, "just giving you a hard time."

Sam felt her friends' eyes on her as X led her out onto the dance floor. Then, with the '40's strains of "Sentimental Journey" sweeping over the floor, X swept Sam along with the music. Not content with a simple box step, they ranged the length of the dance floor, and Sam felt as if she were flying. The swirly white chiffon skirt floated around her as X led her from one complex step to another. Following him felt as natural as breathing.

The song ended with X dipping her, and then both of them turning to the musicians and applauding. Sam wasn't sure, but she thought she saw the bandleader wink at them. Then, the band broke right into a hot rhumba.

"Ready?" X asked Sam.

"Ready!" Sam replied.

They danced the rhumba. And the tango that followed. And another fox-trot. And then another tango. And by the time they finished, there wasn't another couple on the floor. Everyone was at the sidelines, looking on, and grinning. When the final tango finished, the room burst into thunderous applause.

"Take your moment!" X said to Sam, taking her by the hand and spinning her out so that Sam could take a regal bow. X bowed, then they bowed again together, and made their way back to the table. Kurt had arrived sometime during the spontaneous dance exhibition, and he, Emma, and Carrie applauded and whistled when X and Sam got to the table.

"You two were fantastic!" Emma cried, hugging Sam hard.

"Really unbelievable!" Kurt added enthusiastically. "Sam, you are really, really good. I had no idea you were so good."

You're right, Sam thought to herself. *I am good. This is what I'm best at. Not taking care of kids, and not singing rock and roll. This is what I was meant to do.*

And then a thought struck her. Later, when she reflected on it, it was as if a movie had started playing in her head. While Emma and Kurt and Carrie and X jabbered on, Sam was far away, watching the film unroll.

In it were she and X. They were dancing together. They were working together on a dance. They were in front of a huge crowd applauding them. They were choreographing a Broadway show. They were in love, and they were in love with their work.

Sam pulled herself out of her reverie and looked at her friends. Why hadn't she realized it before? The real problem was that she needed to be with a guy who shared

her true passion in life, which was dancing. *That* was why she was so confused!
That was the answer!

Leave it to me, Sam thought wryly, *to
get hooked up with a guy named X. It's too
perfect.*

"Ready to go again?" X asked her.

Sam nodded, smiled again, and let X lead
her out onto the floor.

EIGHT

Sam grinned as she sniffed the flowers sitting on the Jacobses' kitchen counter. They'd been delivered earlier that afternoon while she was out with the twins. Although she'd read the note that had come with the gorgeous arrangement of wildflowers at least a dozen times, she read it once more.

Sandi—
You're a helluva dance partner, Sam. Want to do it again tonight? Same time, same place.

xox
X

X is the coolest, she thought happily. *So original. It is so cool that he deliberately wrote the note to Sandi instead of to Sam. And that he got my address somehow, without me knowing it. I love the idea of a guy who's great at what I'm great at. And such a babe!*

Sam sang to herself happily as she got into one of the Jacobses' cars and drove herself to the recording studio, where the Flirts were scheduled to do two more songs for their demo tape. She felt much more confident and carefree than she had the last time she'd been on her way to the recording studio.

I'm a dancer! she told herself firmly. *That's what I'm really, really good at. The Flirts need me to make the backup dancing look great.*

As Sam drove, she fantasized about going dancing with X that evening, clearing out the dance floor. Even as she walked into the studio, she visualized them on stage in a Broadway show, doing the big duet number, finishing to the roars of the crowd.

She walked nonchalantly into the green room at the studio, and was surprised to see by the clock on the wall that she was actually ten minutes early. Sam was never early. There was one person there already, tuning his guitar.

Pres.

"Hi!" Sam said to him brightly, then belted out the backups to "You Take My Breath Away" to show him that her voice was in good shape.

"Save your voice," Pres said. "You'll need it."

"I'll be fine," Sam assured him. "What's eating you, Mr. Bass Player?"

Pres turned and looked at her closely.

"You," he said finally.

"What are you talking about?"

"You know, Sam," Pres drawled, "it's as if we have a conversation, and then everything I say to you goes in one ear and out the other."

"What do you mean?"

"Didn't we talk two nights ago about commitment?" Pres said, fiddling with the G string on one of the acoustic guitars.

"Oo, the C word," Sam teased.

Pres stared at her coldly and Sam sobered up quickly.

"I was only teasing, I remember—" Sam started to reply.

"Then what the hell were you doing at the country club last night?" Pres confronted her, his dark eyes blazing mad. "This isn't a big island. Did you think I wouldn't find out?"

"Find out what? I went out with Carrie and Emma," Sam said.

"Word has it that you and that guy X were getting awful close for comfort," Pres snorted. "And while usually I don't pay any attention to *word*, with you I've learned that *word* is a lot more honest than you are."

The color drained from Sam's face.

"I *did* go with Carrie and Emma—"

"So what were you doing with X?" Pres asked.

"It's called dancing," Sam snapped. "You know, two people moving together to music? It's legal in all fifty states."

"You seem to be makin' jokes, but I don't seem to be laughin'," Pres drawled, tuning another string on his guitar.

"So, what are you telling me?" Sam

asked. "I'm not supposed to dance with another guy?"

"You can do whatever the hell you want to, girl," Pres replied. "I'm through with it."

Sam felt her hands beginning to shake. "Are you breaking up with me?"

"That'd be a little difficult," Pres shot back, "because that assumes that there's an actual relationship there to be broken up."

"Which there is," Sam replied earnestly. "I just don't like it when you spy on me, because I'm not—"

"Give it a rest, Sam," Pres said in a low voice. His eyes looked both sad and angry. "There's nothing else to say."

Oh damn, Sam said to herself. She felt tears coming to her eyes.

"Look," Sam continued, touching Pres on the arm, "we can work this out, I don't want us to be finished—"

"Well, I do," Pres said evenly. "I thought you'd grow up eventually, but eventually seems like too long to wait. Excuse me, I've got to go talk to the sound engineer."

Pres walked away.

*   *   *

Thirty minutes later, the Flirts were all in the studio, working on the song "Wicked Thing." The guys were laying down the instrumental tracks first, and Sam glanced over at Pres from where she, Emma, and Diana were sitting and waiting.

He doesn't even look upset, she thought to herself, swallowing a lump in her throat. *He's acting as if nothing's happening at all!*

"You okay?" Emma said to her anxiously. "You look pretty pale."

"Fine," Sam whispered back, forcing herself to be upbeat. "Didn't get much beauty sleep last night. You know how I hate that."

"Well," Emma ventured, "you seem sort of down. If you want to talk—"

Sam felt tears threatening but she willed them down. "No, I'm cool," she assured Emma.

"Good," Emma replied, though she didn't look convinced. "What are you doing tonight?"

"Busy," Sam said. "Got a date."

"With Pres?"

"I can't decide what to wear," Sam replied as if she hadn't heard Emma. *I do not want to get into this now with her, because if I do she'll only tell me I'm getting what I deserve, and the next thing that will happen is I'll be crying all over this stupid studio*, Sam told herself.

"Something shocking and decadent sounds good," Emma teased her.

"Always," Sam said, flipping her hair over her shoulders.

"You look like dogmeat," Diana said, coming over to Sam and scrutinizing her face. "And you're getting a zit on your chin."

Sam resisted the urge to place her hands around Diana's neck and squeeze. "I was out partying last night," Sam replied coolly.

"Oh, very bright thing to do the night before we record," Diana replied sarcastically. "Like you don't have enough problems trying to sing after a full night's sleep."

"Diana," Sam said, "you would really do the world a favor if you would just die."

Just then, Pres picked his head up from the charts he'd been studying with the other members of the band across the room.

"Man," he drawled, "is my neck stiff."

Diana looked at Sam, who was pointedly ignoring Pres. Sensing an opportunity, she jumped to her feet and ran over to him.

"I'll rub it for you," Diana volunteered, reaching for Pres.

"That'd be great," Pres said enthusiastically.

Emma looked at Sam with shock on her face. "You're just ignoring that?"

"It's just a backrub," Sam replied laconically. "Let Diana get her little cheap thrill."

Sam held her anger inside as Diana began to knead and massage Pres's neck.

I'm going to kill her, Sam thought to herself. *No, I'm going to beat her up and then I'm going to kill her.*

"That feels good," Pres said with a sigh, as Diana ran her hands down his back.

"I aim to please," Diana replied, now rubbing Pres's shoulder blades. She cast a malicious grin at Sam, who pretended to ignore the whole thing.

Emma looked from Pres and Diana over to Sam and shook her head ruefully.

Val, the sound engineer, stuck his head into the room.

"Time for the backup vocals on 'Wicked Thing,'" he reported.

"I can continue this later, if you'd like," Diana purred to Pres. "Maybe someplace more private."

"We'll see," Pres flirted with her. "We will see."

Diana strutted triumphantly back to her place next to Sam and Emma. Sam was seething. But she was resolved not to show it.

"You seemed to enjoy that," she said to Diana.

"Pres enjoyed it more," Diana retorted.

"Somehow I doubt that," Sam snapped.

"Can we have some quiet out there?" Val called from his place in the booth.

Sam nodded, and slipped her headphones on. In a few seconds, she heard the instrumental tracks for "Wicked Thing." And she started to sing. She was so incensed she sang the wrong notes.

Okay Sam, she told herself, *it can happen to anyone. Just forget about Pres. They'll just do another take and you'll get it right.*

They did another take. And another. And another. And each one, Sam blew just as bad as the one before.

Oh God, Sam thought. *This is turning into a disaster.*

"Sam, can I talk to you?" Billy called to her, after the fourth take was ruined.

"Sure," Sam said, trying to act carefree. She walked over to Billy.

"What's the problem?" he asked her, a pointed edge in his voice.

"Don't know," Sam admitted.

"I need an answer," Billy replied, "so we can try to fix it."

"I said I don't know!" Sam replied, well aware that her bandmates were listening closely to every word.

"Is your mind on this?" Billy asked. "Or is it someplace else?"

"It's here," Sam insisted.

"You sure it's not in Disney World? Or on the dance floor?" Billy asked, his voice cold.

"It's here!" Sam hissed, feeling completely humiliated. "Let's just do it again, dammit."

"Get it right," Billy advised her.

"Yes, sir," Sam replied, a little sarcastically.

She strode back to her place at the microphone. And this time, when the music came through the headphones, Sam got the harmony part absolutely perfect.

"Good job, Sam," Billy said, when the take was over.

"Thanks," Sam said, forcing a grin.

What do I need this for? she thought. *Pres dumps me, Diana moves in, and I'm a dancer, not a singer. They might even kick me out of the band.*

That last thought scared her. But the thought that she had right afterward scared her even more.

If they did, would I really care?

Sam let X lead her by the hand off the dance floor. There was a smattering of applause for them from the few couples in the cocktail lounge at the country club.

Now this is more like it, she thought happily. *This is where I'm supposed to be.*

She'd suffered through the rest of the session, making a few more mistakes. Then, she'd refused to go out to the Play Café with Emma, telling her friend that she needed to be alone for a while. Emma had pressed her a bit, and then left Sam alone. After she got back to the Jacobs' house, she sleepwalked through her evening routine with the twins until it was time for her date with X. Finally, she got to the club, to X, to the only place where she felt truly at home—on the dance floor.

"You're really wonderful," X said appreciatively after they'd settled in at a small table near the back of the room.

"To know me is to love me," Sam grinned at him, stretching out her long legs and rubbing her calfs.

"Sore?" X asked.

"Just a little," Sam smiled. "I'm not used to such a good partner."

"Me neither," X mused, running his right

hand through his mussed blond hair. "So, Sam, tell me about yourself. Where'd you learn to dance like that?"

Sam started talking. And after a while the subject was no longer dancing, but what it was like growing up the elder of two sisters from Junction, Kansas.

Oh my God, she thought to herself with embarrassment, *I'm going on and on. I must be boring him to death. Sam, get a grip!*

But X was paying close attention.

"Your real ambition is to dance?" he asked her.

"Absolutely," Sam replied, taking a sip of the club soda she'd ordered.

"Well," X reflected, "you can do it. You've got the talent. The question is how badly you want it."

"More than anything in the world," Sam said truthfully.

"Well . . ." X began, and stopped to think a moment. "Oh hell, I shouldn't spring this on you like this—"

"Spring what?" Sam asked.

"It's just that I'm thinking about taking

my act on the road," X said, "and I'm going to need a partner."

"So?"

"So, maybe you're her," X suggested.

Sam had her club soda halfway to her lips and she stopped it there, then put it down.

"Me?"

X nodded.

"Me, Sam Bridges?"

"Or you, Sandi Bridges," X replied with a laugh.

Sam forced herself to be calm. "What did you have in mind?"

X outlined a plan where he and his partner would create and choreograph their own act, begin to perform in such places as Lake Tahoe, California, and the Catskills of New York, and then take it to Las Vegas and Atlantic City.

"What about your dance company?" Sam asked, suddenly a bit suspicious. She'd once been completely duped by a dance company that had promised her a job overseas, and the company turned out to be a cover for prostitution.

"No problem," X said. "They'll fly us back to California, I'll choreograph, and then it's back out on the road."

"And you think I might be the right partner for you," Sam repeated.

"Could be," X smiled. "Fred Astaire had Ginger Rogers, and she did everything he did backward . . . and in high heels! So, why not X and Sam?"

Why not, indeed? Sam thought to herself. *Why not?*

"I'll have to think about it," Sam said finally. This was not a decision she wanted to rush, but when she thought about it, maybe all the bad things that had been happening to her lately, and all the problems with Danny and Pres, were a sign that *this* was what she should do!

"You do that," X said. "In the meantime, would you care to dance?"

"Love to," Sam replied, taking X's outstretched hand, which had begun to feel very comfortable in hers.

And she meant it, with every bone in her dance-crazed body.

NINE

"I'm going to work on my tan," Allie announced, pushing her chair away from the breakfast table the next morning.

"Well, that's dumb—you've already got a sunburn," Becky remarked, finishing her glass of milk. "Sam, tell Allie it's dumb."

"What?" Sam asked dreamily, lost in reliving her dancing triumph with X the night before.

"I *said* Allie has a sunburn and she's going out to tan," Becky repeated impatiently.

Sam finally focussed on Allie. "That's not a good idea."

Allie gave her a withering look, held up some 15-level sunscreen so Sam could see it, and flounced out of the house.

Sam began to clear up the breakfast

dishes. To her utter shock, Becky joined her in carrying dishes from the table.

"Sam?" Becky asked, twirling a lock of her long dark hair in her fingers, "can I ask you something?"

"Sure," Sam replied, as she rinsed the dishes and stuck them in the dishwasher.

"Well," Becky said, leaning against the counter, "it's kind of, sort of . . . personal."

"Okay," Sam said. *Please don't let her ask me about sex,* Sam thought to herself. *Of course, Becky probably knows more about it than I do.*

"It's about guys," Becky said.

"Uh huh," Sam replied. She closed the dishwasher and sat back down at the kitchen table. "Well, guys *are* my favorite subject."

"Mine too," Becky said earnestly, trying to bond with Sam. "The thing is, since guys are all over you I figured you'd know what I should do."

"Really?" Sam asked, taken aback by this comment. Allie and Becky usually spent so much time insulting her she could hardly believe Becky really thought she was popular with guys. *Even though, of course, I am*, Sam added to herself.

Becky nodded and came to sit with Sam. "Pres, Danny, even X—they're all after you!"

"Well, yeah," Sam said, loathe to admit to Becky that she had guy problems. "But it's not that simple—"

"I wish you'd just listen to me," Becky said earnestly.

"Okay, I will," Sam promised. "Go ahead."

"It's Ian," Becky began.

"Ian Templeton?" Sam asked.

"Of course Ian Templeton," Becky said impatiently. "Are there any other Ians on the island?"

Sam had to admit she didn't know any.

"Well, the thing is, I like him a lot," Becky admitted.

"That's . . . a change, isn't it?" Sam asked carefully. Ian had long had a crush on Becky, but Becky never seemed to return the compliment.

"Maybe," Becky said, picking some nail

polish off her pinky. "But I'm allowed to change my mind!"

"Absolutely," Sam agreed.

"I mean, I used to think he was just a kid, you know?" Becky continued. "And, well, this is gross—but when he first asked me to be in the band I only did it because his dad is a big rock star."

Sam nodded noncomittally.

"Anyway, now I know how cool Ian really is—he's a real artist. And Allie is giving me a really hard time about it."

"Maybe she's jealous," Sam suggested.

"No way," Becky said. "Allie is such a child—she thinks only some beefcake-type stud can be cute. Well, I've matured beyond that!"

Sam nodded.

"Here's the thing," Becky continued in a low, serious voice. "I don't think Ian really likes me."

"So, who's the bigger problem, Allie or Ian?" Sam asked.

"Both!" Becky cried. "But mostly Ian. He ignores me!"

"Are you sure?"

"Of course I'm sure," Becky snorted. "Why else would I be talking to you?"

"Because sometimes guys don't show on the outside what they're thinking on the inside," Sam explained, thinking about how Danny played it so close to the vest with her when they were in Florida, even though she found out later how much he cared for her.

"Not Ian," Becky said fervently. "He's an artist. He's so much cooler than guys even older than him. So much deeper, you know?"

Sam nodded, indicating that Becky should go on.

"And the way he handled that bad article about him in *Rock On* magazine—wow!" Becky continued, now on a roll. "He is the coolest."

It's the real thing, Sam thought to herself. *She's head over heels, even though last summer she treated him like dirt.*

"You know those poems I was writing the other night?" Becky asked.

"Um-hmmm."

"They were for Ian," Becky said shyly.

"But he doesn't even pay attention to me anymore."

"Well, I think Ian has always liked you," Sam replied.

"What, as a friend?" Becky wondered sadly.

"More, I think," Sam said.

"So then why isn't he paying any attention to me?" Becky cried. "Do you think I should give him the poems I wrote?"

"That might be a little overwhelming," Sam considered.

"So then, what do I do?" Becky moaned. "I can't stop thinking about him!"

"Well, I'd say take it slow," Sam advised. "I mean, he's here on the island, and you're on the island, and no one is going anywhere, so give it time."

"I hate giving things time!" Becky ranted. "I want things to happen now!"

"Yeah, I know the feeling," Sam agreed with a smile. "But that's still my best advice to you."

"Okay," Becky said with a sigh. "But it sucks, if you ask me."

"And don't pressure yourself or him,"

Sam warned Becky, ignoring that last comment. "Because he might not be ready, and there's nothing a person who isn't ready hates more than being pressured."

Sounds like good advice, Sam said to herself, as she was delivering it. *If only it was that easy to give advice to myself, or to take it from my friends!*

"Sam! Letter for you!" Allie Jacobs called up the stairs to Sam, who was in her room getting dressed after her Dear Abby session with Becky.

Sam poked her head out of her door as Allie came bounding up the stairs with an envelope in her hand.

"What did you tell Becky?" Allie asked curiously.

"None of your business," Sam replied, putting her hand out for her letter.

"It's from Danny," Allie replied, holding the envelope out of Sam's reach. "What did you tell my stupid sister?"

"Look, if Becky wants you to know, she'll tell you herself," Sam said with irritation. She grabbed for Danny's letter and snagged the edge, pulling it out of Allie's hand.

"It was about Ian, I bet," Allie smirked. "I think Ian's a dweeb."

"Your sister obviously doesn't," Sam said.

"So, she's wrong," Allie replied with a shrug.

"There's really no reason for you to tease Becky about this," Sam said reasonably. "It just makes her feel bad."

"Sure, that's the whole point," Allie said cheerfully.

"But that's mean," Sam pointed out. "Does it make you happy to be mean?"

Allie shifted her weight and folded her arms. "Well, she's always so busy mooning around over Ian that she doesn't even have time for me," Allie said defensively. "Like, we were supposed to go shopping at the Cheap Boutique, but Becky had to write a love poem. Then we were supposed to go to the movies with Brenda, but Becky had to stay here in case Ian called. It's obnoxious!"

Oh, so that's it! Sam realized. *Allie is jealous that Ian is taking up Becky's time!*

"Well, if Becky has plans with you and breaks them, she's being inconsiderate and you should call her on it," Sam advised.

Allie looked at her suspiciously. "How come you sound like an adult, all of a sudden?"

"I do?" Sam asked.

Allie nodded.

"I'm just trying to help," Sam replied.

Allie gave her a pained look. "I still think Ian is a lame-oid," she concluded and turned on her heel.

Well, that did no good at all, Sam thought as she watched Allie run down the stairs. *And besides, I'm probably the last person who should be giving anyone any advice about anything.*

Sam looked down at the letter in her hand, went into her room, and flopped down on her bed. Her heart beat a little faster as she tore it open. Allie was right—it was from Danny.

Sam,
I'm writing this to you on the bus up to Ellsworth, so sorry for the squiggly

133

writing. Can't help it. I had a wonderful time with you. I felt as though on this trip we really connected—we were always special friends, but I thought this time we came together a lot closer than we ever did before. I really do think that you are great. We all have problems and complicated lives—even me!—but I feel now that if we go at these problems together we can really make something great. We have so much in common—we're even both Jewish! So, I don't know how to say this easily, so I'll go ahead and say it simply: I'm willing if you are. I love you. Please say yes.

Danny

Great, Sam thought, *just great. Why does everyone have to be falling in love with me all at once? And what's going to happen if I tell Danny I'm not ready to make a commitment to him—is he going to end his friendship with me too? Why can't these guys be more like X? He's such a cool guy, he's no pressure—none at all.*

Sam heard Dan Jacobs get back from his early morning golf game. She went downstairs to greet him.

"Hi Sam," he said, taking off the baseball cap he was wearing. "How've my girls been?"

Allie's been obnoxious and Becky's in need of a good psychotherapist, Sam wanted to respond, but instead she just said, "They're fine."

"Great," Dan said. "I shot eighty-seven today." He was beaming.

"Great, Mr. Jacobs," Sam responded, though she could care less how he golfed, and had no idea what shooting an eighty-seven meant.

"Hey, I've told you and told you, call me Dan," Mr. Jacobs told Sam. He looked at his watch. "Uh, listen, Sam, are the girls here?"

"Upstairs," Sam replied.

"Well, I have a . . . friend coming over, and I thought Tabitha—my friend—and I would take the girls out for ice cream or something. You want a couple of hours off?"

"That would be great, thanks," Sam

135

replied, always eager for time off. "Uh, do the girls know about this 'friend'?"

"No," Dan admitted. "But I think they'll really like Tabitha. She's very special."

Yeah, right, Sam thought. *Mr. Jacobs springs his little playmates on the girls and the girls always react badly. Why doesn't he ever learn? But hey, it's his life, not mine.*

"Well, I'll just go call my friends, then," Sam said. "Thanks again." She went to the phone to call Emma and Carrie, to see if they were free to go to the beach. *And to give me some guy advice,* she added in her own mind. *I need it a lot more than Becky!* But when she dialed Emma at the Hewitts and Carrie at the Templetons, neither of them were home.

Fine, Sam thought, feeling a little miffed even though she knew both her friends were working. *I'll go by myself.*

She went upstairs, put a bathing suit on under her T-shirt and shorts, and then borrowed one of Dan's cars to drive to the beach.

Walking along the main beach by herself, Sam tried to sort out her options. But the more she thought, the more confused she got.

X wants me to go out on the road with him, to do this dance thing with him. It's what I want to do, and I really like him— he is such a babe—but I don't really know him all that well, she told herself as she walked, paying no attention to the scenery around her.

But things are going from bad to worse, another voice said to her. *Why bother? You've outgrown this place. Guys are pressuring you and they're not taking your feelings into account, are they? First Pres, now Danny—what do you need it for? It's just holding you back from what you really want to do, right?*

You're a quitter, another voice said to her. *Your singing is going downhill, you're afraid you're not really good enough to be in the band, and you're having problems with Pres, so all you want to do is run away. Like a big baby. That's all you are, Sam. A big baby. What about Emma and Carrie? What about your job?*

Yeah, but it's better to leave than to be

137

humiliated, still another voice said to her. *They're going to kick you out of the band, especially now that Pres has broken up with you. You want to hang around and face that humiliation?*

By the time Sam had reached the end of the main beach and then walked slowly back, it seemed that she had rolled her situation over in her mind so many times that it had turned into a big glob of mush.

She stood on the beach, picked up a shell and threw it out into the water. She felt very confused, and very alone.

Later that day, as Sam was in the Jacobs kitchen starting to prepare dinner for the family, the phone rang.

"Jacobs residence," Sam answered wearily. She was exhausted from all her mental anguish.

"Hey Sam," a familiar male voice said, "it's Billy."

That familiar knot formed again in Sam's stomach. There could only be one reason for Billy to be calling her—trouble.

"Hi Billy," Sam said, trying to be nonchalant. "What's up, cowboy?"

"I don't have much time," Billy replied, "because I'm going into the studio to help mix a couple of songs. But I wanted to talk to you."

"Here I am," Sam replied lightly.

"About the last session," Billy continued.

"I didn't sound so great, huh?" Sam laughed. "But then I got it together."

"You're gonna have to get it together on your own time," Billy said tersely. "Not on band time. How long did you warm up before you came in?"

"Uh, some," Sam hedged, even though the truth was she hadn't warmed up at all. She'd been too busy worrying about her life.

"We're a professional band," Billy responded. "You act like a pro or you're out. That means warming up and vocalizing before you get into the studio."

What's he really saying here? Sam said to herself, anger rising in her. *Emma never warms up before she sings. Neither does Diana. I bet Pres just got him to call me because Pres wants me out of the Flirts!*

Sam decided to be direct. She felt like she had nothing to lose.

"Did Pres tell you to call me—"

Billy's voice cut her off instantly. "What happened or happens between you and Pres or between you and any guy is your own business," Billy stated. "I care about the music. That's that."

"But what do you think of—"

"Sam," and here Billy's voice grew steely, "do you think this is the first time that a romance between two people in a band has gone belly up? It happens all the time. That's rock and roll."

"It's not totally over," Sam remonstrated. "Did Pres say it was totally over?"

"That's between the two of you," Billy responded. "What I care about right now is the recording session. And I'm advising you to get your act together."

"Gee, thanks for the support," Sam said, feeling hurt.

"Sam, this isn't a joke," Billy said finally, and hung up the phone without even saying good-bye.

Sam just stood there, holding the phone.

Then she finally put down the receiver. *Billy is supposed to be my friend*, she thought miserably, *but now that Pres broke up with me it's like he could care less. They probably all want me out of the band but they can't figure out how to do it. They probably want a better singer than me.*

Sam trudged over to the refrigerator and began taking out stuff for salad, her head spinning. *I am not going to hang around just so I can get fired and humiliated in front of everyone—in front of Diana! Wouldn't she love that! They think I have nothing else to do but sing backup in their band? No way!*

Tears were streaming down Sam's cheeks, but she brushed them away angrily. Before she could stop herself, she ran up to her room, took the piece of paper that X had given her the other night with his phone number on it, went to her phone, and dialed his number.

"X X X," X answered the phone, his voice light and full of charm.

"Hi X," Sam said. "It's me, Sam Bridges."

"Hey, good to hear from you," X said.

141

"How's my favorite dance partner?"

"Great," Sam said, ignoring the awful sick feeling in her stomach. "Hopefully, I'm about to be your permanent dance partner. What you told me about the other night? I'm in. One hundred percent in."

TEN

"We feel like we haven't seen you in days," Carrie said, smearing sunscreen on her arms.

"We're really glad you called us," Emma added, reaching for her own sunscreen tube. It was another glorious Maine day, and the noonday temperature was definitely heating up.

"Hey, what are friends for?" Sam replied lightly. "What do you think of the suit? I borrowed it from Becky—we are actually getting along this week." She jumped to her feet and spun around, showing off the acid-green bikini with the mesh sides.

"On you, hot," Carrie nodded approvingly. "On me, disaster."

"Wrong—you could wear it and Billy

would be a drooling fool," Sam said, "but you just don't."

I'm stalling, Sam thought, *and I don't know why. I know I told X last night that I was going to quit the Flirts and go out on his dance tour with him, but I just don't want to tell my friends. They'll be so pissed at me!*

"So what's this big news you've got for us?" Carrie asked. "You planning to quit your job and move to Paris?"

"Not exactly—" Sam began slowly.

"I know!" Emma chimed in. "You are having a sex-change operation and are planning to write a tell-all book about what it really feels like to be a guy!"

Carrie laughed. "Very sick, Emma, I like it!"

"You guys, I—" Sam tried again.

"Wait, wait, how about this!" Carrie yelped. "She's going to marry both Pres and Danny, and the three of them are going to live together in a phone booth in Junction, Kansas!"

Emma and Carrie cracked up laughing. So hard, in fact, that for a time, they didn't notice Sam sitting there expressionless.

Then, they did notice.

"What's wrong?" Emma said with concern.

"Gosh, I didn't mean to hurt your—"

It's now or never, Sam thought grimly, her head a whirlwind of emotions. *God, I feel like such a quitter. Why do I feel so bad about this?*

Sam waved them off. "It isn't that, it's just that, well—"

Sam watched her friends lean toward her with concern written all over their faces. *How can I actually be doing this?* she said to herself, again. *These are the best friends I've ever had!*

"Yes?" Emma prompted her.

"I'm quitting the Flirts," Sam said quickly, figuring that the best way to say it was to just get it out. "X asked me to go out on tour with him on a dance gig and I said yes."

There, I've done it. Now let's wait for the sawdust to hit the fan, Sam thought unhappily. *Why don't I feel better about this, now that I've told my best friends the truth? This could really be the big break I'm looking for. Why do I feel so awful?*

Emma and Carrie sat a moment, stunned. Then they looked at each other, and broke up laughing. Carrie got up as if she were a zombie, walked stiff-legged over to the pool, and fell in backward, even though she was still wearing shorts, a T-shirt, and sunglasses. This made Emma crack up even more.

Sam sat there, stone-faced.

"Sam, you kill me!" Carrie called from the pool, still laughing.

"That is too funny, Sam!" Emma exclaimed.

I feel awful, Sam thought. *I can always say it was a joke and back out. Yeah, that's what I'm going to do.*

And then another voice inside her said, *Oh no, you are going to go through with this. Remember why you are doing it. Do you want to be humiliated and rejected again?*

Sam felt a lump form in her throat. She fought it back.

"Yeah, you're kidding, right, Sam?"

Carrie said, trying to wring water out of her shirt as she walked back toward Sam and Emma.

"Sorry," Sam said, as lightly as she could. "Samantha Bridges is outta here!"

"Sam, you're taking this joke too far," Carrie said, a frown starting to furrow her brow. "Please be serious."

"Come on, Sam," Emma added, echoing Carrie's tone.

"How much more serious can I be?" Sam asked, her voice cracking a bit with emotion. "I am quitting the band, and X asked me to join him on a big national tour. Which I am going to do. And that's that." Then she told Emma and Carrie the whole story of how X came to ask her to be his dance partner.

When she was done, Emma and Carrie sat in stunned silence.

"But why?" Carrie cried. Actual tears were starting to form in the corners of her eyes.

"The band," Emma surmised, a bit coldly. "It's because she had a couple of bad nights with the band. What she doesn't realize is

147

that it happens to everyone, even big stars. And they don't quit."

"It's not that," Sam said defensively.

"Really?" Emma asked in a frosty voice, obviously not convinced.

"This is a huge opportunity," Sam tried to reason with them.

"Yeah," Emma scoffed uncharacteristically. "An opportunity for you to leave the band and your two best friends in the lurch."

"You think I shouldn't do it?" Sam asked her, point-blank. "And miss the chance?"

"That's right," Carrie said emphatically. "I think you are out of your mind."

"Look Sam," Emma added, leaning forward, "so what if you had some problems in the studio. You don't have to be the best at everything you do, you know—"

"Why not, you are," Sam shot back at Emma.

Emma's face reddened. "I don't think that's true," she said in a low voice.

"Oh, Emma, you're perfect and everyone knows it," Sam said.

"That is not true, but we aren't talking

about me," Emma said evenly. "Have you even talked this over with Pres?"

"How could I? He broke up with me." Sam blurted out, tears coming to her eyes.

Emma and Carrie stared at Sam.

"He—" Carrie began.

"That's right," Sam interrupted. "He broke up with me. We are through. Done. Over. History."

"And that's why you're quitting?" Emma asked.

"I told you," Sam said in a hardened voice. "I'm quitting to pursue what I really should have been doing all along."

"But . . . don't you think you just need to think this over a while longer?" Carrie asked plaintively.

"No," Sam said, suddenly feeling stubborn. "My mind is made up, and that's that."

"Have you told Billy yet?" Carrie asked.

"No," Sam admitted.

"Then you can still change your mind!" Emma cried.

"But I'm not going to," Sam stated, feeling her resolve stiffen.

Why won't they support me? she thought to herself. *Why won't they just look at things from my point of view, for a change?*

"Well," Emma said, her tone turning a little icy. "I think this is totally uncalled for."

"I'm just going to miss her," Carrie said to Emma, emotion filling her voice.

"Hey, lighten up," Sam bantered. "We'll still be best friends!"

"Yeah, right," Carrie blurted. "You're off dancing with some guy you hardly know, and we're here, babysitting."

"You got to admit, Sam," Emma said, "things are going to change big-time."

"That's true," Sam responded, "but it doesn't mean that we won't be best friends."

"That's easy for you to say," Carrie said sadly.

"I wouldn't even be in the stupid Flirts if it wasn't for you," Emma said suddenly. "And now, you're quitting!"

"That's not true!" Sam retorted.

"Yes it is!" Emma cried.

And then Sam realized it was true. *It*

was me who told Emma to go and audi-tion. It was me who encouraged her. She was the one who didn't want to do it. And now she's going to be in the band all by her-self. Correction. She'll be a backup singer with Diana, Sam thought.

"Well, things change," Sam said.

"This isn't things changing," Emma re-plied. "This is *you* changing. And I think you're making a big mistake."

"Sam, stop and think!" Carrie cried. "You think you're the only person in the world who's got mixed-up feelings about a cou-ple of guys? Because in my opinion that's what this is all about."

"I agree with Carrie," Emma said.

"It's not that—" Sam began.

"Come on, Sam," Carrie pleaded with her. "Who do you think you're kidding? We're your best friends. We see what's going on."

"You can think what you want—" Sam said defensively.

"Look," Emma said, "you think Kurt and I don't fight all the time? Because we do. I hate to admit it, but we do. You think

I don't remember what happened out in California with your brother Adam? You think I don't stay up nights because Kurt keeps pressuring me to get engaged?"

"And me," Carrie chimed in, "you think it was easy splitting with Josh? You think I sometimes don't lie in bed at night and wonder if I did the right thing? You think I don't worry that I made the biggest mistake of my life?"

"This is different!" Sam said.

"Not so much," Emma said sadly. "Not so much at all."

"Running away is not going to solve your problems, Sam," Carrie said softly.

"I'm not running away!" Sam insisted, but once again tears came to her eyes.

"That's a matter of opinion," Emma replied.

"Well, thanks for nothing!" Sam said angrily.

"How did you think we were going to react?" Emma said hotly.

"I'd thought you'd be my friends!" Sam answered.

"We are your friends," Carrie said simply.

"That's why we're upset. So what exactly is your plan?"

Sam sketched briefly for Emma and Carrie the plan that she and X had worked out on the phone the previous evening. X was going to stay on the island until the end of the summer and rehearse in a local dance studio with Sam, so that Sam wouldn't have to quit her job. Then, at the end of the summer, they would go for their first gig in Nevada.

"Well," Emma said finally, "that's better than you leaving tomorrow, which is what I expected."

"Me too," Carrie added. "Sorry I got so upset before. I thought this was it."

"Apologies accepted," Sam said with as much grace as she could muster.

"I'm still going to try to talk you out of this," Carrie stated. "For a little while, anyway."

"My mind is made up."

"That doesn't mean you can't change it," Emma said. "We have that privilege."

"When are you going to tell Billy?" Carrie

asked Sam. "Because he's going to be really pissed."

"You're wrong," Sam said flatly. "He is going to be relieved." *Because now he won't have to fire me,* she added to herself. "I'll call him this afternoon."

"He won't be relieved," Emma said with a sigh. "And please remember, you can change your mind between now and that phone call."

"I'm not going to," Sam answered. "I'm a dancer and I should be dancing. That's pretty simple."

Emma and Carrie looked at her with total disbelief in their eyes.

They don't think I'm telling the truth, she thought. *Well, am I?*

"So," X asked Sam as she walked into Sunset Dance Concepts on Main Street downtown, "you ready to rehearse?"

"Sure am," Sam answered, mustering her best smile.

"You clear everything with your friends in the band?" X asked her directly.

"Sure did," Sam responded, slinging her

dance bag into the corner of the studio.

"How'd they take it?"

"Fine," Sam said. "They're professionals. Besides, backup singers are a dime a dozen."

And if I were Pinocchio, my nose would be stretching into Canada just about now, Sam thought. *Actually, it was a disaster. Billy spoke to me for about five seconds and said that he saw it coming and that he wasn't surprised, considering my past attitude. And when I asked Pres to come to the phone so I could tell him, he wouldn't even talk to me.* Sam gulped hard. She still felt the terrible pain she'd felt when Billy told her Pres wouldn't come to the phone.

"Great!" X said, "then we can get right to work, with no distractions."

"I'm ready," Sam said as confidently as she could.

X didn't hear her, because he was busy fiddling with a cassette in the portable player he had brought. The music started up—it was an upbeat, rocking number.

"Now," X said, "watch exactly what I do."

Sam tried to follow the routine that X

was laying out in the studio for her. But though she watched his every move, what she was really seeing were the faces of her friends, all looking sad and angry, all staring back at her.

ELEVEN

"Terrific!" X yelled, as he and Sam hit the final pose of their routine. "Let's take five."

Sam plopped down on the makeshift couch in the studio, out of breath. They had been rehearsing for three hours.

What a routine! she thought to herself. *I'm sure not at Disney World anymore. I think we got a lot of good work done. At least X seems happy.*

As if to confirm her thoughts, X walked over to Sam with a big grin on his face, holding two chilled bottles of Gatorade. He handed one to her, and she took it gratefully.

"Cheers," X said, still smiling.

"That's what I want," Sam replied. "Thousands of them."

"We're on the way," X replied, settling himself down on the couch.

"I'm beat," Sam admitted.

"But it's a good feeling, right?" X asked, throwing back some Gatorade.

"Yeah," Sam admitted. "It is."

"That's how you know you're a real dancer," X replied. "You thrive on that feeling. And you are absolutely a real dancer, Sam."

Sam grinned happily at the compliment. *Take that Billy and Pres and everybody. I'm a dancer! A real dancer! No one's saying I'm holding them back in this studio!*

"I love it," Sam said simply.

"So do I," X replied. "There's nothing really like it."

"One thing, maybe," Sam replied flirtatiously, though she really didn't intend to. *It just popped out of my mouth,* she thought wickedly.

"Waking up on a January morning in Minnesota and remembering that you have an eighth grade algebra test you forgot to study for," X said longingly. "Now, that's my idea of a peak experience."

Sam laughed. "Is that where you grew up? Minnesota?"

"Yep," X replied, taking a big drink from his bottle. "Southern Minnesota, near Mankato."

"A huge dance center," Sam said solemnly.

"A huge algebra center," X responded.

"So how long did you survive there?" Sam queried.

"Long enough to know I had to get out," X replied.

"Sounds a lot like me and Kansas," Sam mused, taking a sip of Gatorade and rubbing her right calf gingerly to prevent it from cramping up.

X looked over at Sam. "You didn't exactly fit in, huh?"

"That's the understatement of the century," Sam said. "I felt like some kind of Martian or something."

"Yeah, I know that feeling," X said, staring into the distance.

"Every day of high school was like some kind of torture," Sam continued earnestly.

"So, you're telling me you weren't popular?" X asked, his eyebrows raised. "Not Little Miss Popularity? Not Homecoming Queen?"

"Please," Sam scoffed. "I had barely outgrown my childhood nickname—Stork. And the guys at my high school were sooooo awful. The biggest club at my school was Future Farmers of America."

X threw his head back and laughed heartily. "Somehow I don't picture you plowing the back forty."

"No kidding," Sam agreed with a grin. "Even my sister, Ruth Ann—who is, like, this major brain—joined Future Homemakers!"

"Gruesome," X shuddered dramatically. "My youngest sister, Lark, won the Betty Crocker Bake-Off last year! Everyone in my family is still bragging about it!"

"Then you know just what I'm talking about!" Sam exclaimed. "Everyone back in Junction is just so . . . so small town and conservative—especially my family. Is your family like that?"

"Absolutely," X said. "I come from this big Norwegian Lutheran clan—four sisters and two brothers. They have a tendency to reproduce at a rapid clip, which is not exactly in my plans!"

"Mine, either!" Sam agreed fervently.

"I'm the black sheep," X said, looking at Sam very directly. "The blackest. If my parents really understood me, they'd probably disown me."

"I know that feeling," Sam replied with feeling. "I've felt that way all my life."

"A lot of dancers do," X said, reaching over to give Sam's hand a squeeze. "Listen, you're talented, you're special. That's really something in this world."

"Thanks," Sam said, smiling at X.

"It's going to be tough work," X warned her.

"I'll do it," Sam promised.

As long as you're the one I'm doing it with, she thought to herself, *I'll be fine. Just fine.*

Sam got back to the Jacobses at about eleven o'clock that night. She found a note by her bed that had been left by Becky, telling her that Danny Franklin had called from Florida, and that she should call him right away.

That's weird, Sam thought, puzzled. *I thought Danny was out canoeing someplace in the wilderness. Well, I was going to have to tell him eventually that I'm going out on tour with X. It's just going to have to be sooner rather than later. I hope he doesn't freak out.*

Before she could lose her nerve, she went to the phone and dialed Danny's number in Orlando.

"Hello?"

"Hey, it's Sam. What are you doing in Florida?"

"We ran into trouble on the river," Danny reported. "My friend got stung by a bee."

"So?" Sam asked. "No biggie."

"Not unless you're allergic. Which he is."

"So what happened?"

"They flew him to Bangor," Danny explained. "And I got a flight back to Florida."

"Wow," Sam exclaimed. "I didn't know a person could be that allergic to bees!"

"Neither did I, actually," Danny said.

"So, is he okay?"

"Yeah," Danny said. "But he's bummed out that we didn't get to do our canoeing trip, and so am I."

"Oh," Sam replied, suddenly feeling uncomfortable.

"I got your letter," Danny said, finally. "It made me really happy."

"Oh," Sam said again.

"You okay?" Danny asked.

"Oh yeah, fine!" Sam replied. "A little tired."

"I liked your suggestion," Danny murmured.

My suggestion? What did I suggest? At the moment, Sam couldn't remember what she'd written in her note to Danny just a few days before.

"Oh yeah?" she ventured.

"So," Danny said, "I'm already making plans to come back to Maine, like you said. I figure in about three weeks I'll have things together enough."

Oh damn, Sam thought. *He can't come here now!*

"I don't know if that's such a good idea, Danny," Sam said slowly. "I'm kind of busy now."

"Oh, that's okay," Danny said easily. "I know you have to work. But we'll have a blast anyway. Besides, your boss loves me, remember?"

Sam took a deep breath. There was silence on the phone.

"You okay?" Danny asked again. "You're not pulling a Sam on me again, are you?"

Pulling a Sam? Sam thought.

"What's that?"

"A Sam . . ." Danny began, "wait, let me look up the dictionary definition on that. Ah, here it is. It says 'A Sam is when Sam Bridges gets impetuous about something and it makes her change all her plans that she made but then she gets real upset about the change in plans and then her friend Danny gets hurt.'"

Sam felt as if someone were twisting her guts around. Danny was so sweet, so terrific, how *could* she hurt him?

"Well, things have changed a little," Sam said slowly, hating herself even as the words came out of her mouth.

She heard Danny take a breath like he'd been punched in the stomach. For a moment, there was nothing but silence on the phone.

"Okay," Danny said. "Give it to me straight. Don't beat around the bush."

So Sam told Danny the whole story of her problem with the band—leaving out the part about Pres—and about how X had asked her to go out on tour with him in the fall.

"So what does that have to do with anything?" Danny asked, once Sam had finished. "You're going to be rehearsing on the island. I'll come see you."

Silence.

Finally Danny spoke again. "Sam, are you involved with this guy X? Or getting involved with him?"

"No," Sam replied, telling herself she was telling the truth.

"But you want to," Danny said, rather than asked.

"I don't know," Sam answered, feeling anxious and guilty, as if something had already happened with X.

"Well," Danny said finally, "I should have known."

"Nothing's happened!" Sam insisted. "I mean, we're just dance partners!"

"Hey, you can't fight the feeling," Danny said in a sad voice.

Sam felt all the fear, frustration, and anger of the past few days well up inside her. She tried to shove it back down, but she couldn't. She exploded at Danny.

"What do you mean, I can't fight the feeling?" she yelled. "You think I'm a total slut and fall for every guy that comes along? I'm not married to you, I'm not even engaged to you!"

"Who said anything about that?" Danny shouted back. "You're just lashing out at me so you won't have to look at yourself in the mirror, Sam!"

"That's not true, I—"

"I'm the one who knows you, remember?" Danny interrupted. "I think you're just running away again—from the band, from me, from anything that could hurt you."

"No!" Sam insisted. "I—"

"You can't run forever, Sam. 'Cuz one day you'll run so far from everyone who loves you that there won't be anyone there to help pick up the pieces when you fall. Good-bye, Sam."

Danny hung up on her.

Okay, so what, I don't care, Sam told herself, still staring at the phone. *Why does every guy think that just because you don't want some big commitment that you must be running from something? X is the only one who isn't like that. I'm free, fine, and feisty, so who cares?*

She stomped into the bathroom, took a quick shower, and then went to her closet and selected a straight black lycra minidress. She pulled on her red cowboy boots, put on some makeup, and stuck her hair up on her head with a black ribbon. Then she pulled on a black velvet baseball cap—backwards—and headed downstairs. She borrowed one of Dan Jacobs's cars (he had given her permission earlier, of course, since he was out with the twins and Tabatha) and drove to the Play Café.

The Café, per usual, was hopping. Sam

167

walked in, said hello to a few people she knew, and wended her way toward the back. She was half-hoping that Emma or Carrie would be there, but was dreading seeing them at the same time.

Suddenly, she spotted two people she knew.

But it wasn't Emma and Carrie.

It was X. And sitting across from him at a tiny table was Diana De Witt.

Then X spotted her. And motioned Sam to join them.

What's he doing here with Diana? Sam thought, starting to feel angry all over again.

"Hey partner," X said to her warmly, scootching over a bit so Sam would have more room to sit down.

"Hey quitter," Diana said lightly. "Nice to have you out of the band, but I was hoping you'd be gone from my life."

"Diana," X said lightly, "shut up. You just don't recognize that a person has to follow her dream."

Wow, Sam thought to herself. *They must*

not be together, otherwise he'd never say that kind of thing to her.

"You two come here together?" Sam asked.

"Yes," Diana said quickly.

"No," X replied. "Diana wishes we'd come here together, though," he added with a teasing grin.

"Can you blame me?" Diana asked, sensuously stretching her arm out and brushing it against X's own tanned arm.

"Learn to dance," X joked with her, "and then maybe you'll have a chance." He winked at Sam, who felt a thrill race through her body.

"I happen to be a great dancer," Diana replied testily. "I think you meant to say Sam should learn to sing, but I guess that's asking for the impossible."

"Sam's a dancer, not a singer," X said, taking a sip of the martini he had ordered earlier.

"Everyone is glad you quit, you know," Diana continued maliciously, staring at Sam. "Everyone is saying how you were holding us back."

Sam felt as if knives were digging into her heart. "Well, now everyone is happy," she said, forcing a careless tone.

"Absolutely," Diana agreed. "I can't wait until the auditions for your replacement. They should be really fun! And I'm sure we'll find someone who can actually sing this time!"

I'm going to kill her, that's all, Sam thought. She rose out of her chair, but X put a restraining hand on her arm.

Diana spotted a tall, rangy guy coming into the Café.

"Excuse me," she said to X and Sam. "That's William McWilliams, the actor who's on that soap. He wants to meet me."

"Then by all means, to the attack, Diana!" X encouraged her. Diana left, and X and Sam cracked up.

"That girl always manages to push my buttons," Sam grimaced.

"Only if you let her," X replied.

"More easily said than done," Sam admitted. She looked around for the waitress. "I'm starved. Want to order a pizza?"

X laughed. "I don't know about you, but I put on weight if I eat pizza at night."

"Not me," Sam told him. "In fact, I have to eat pizza at night to keep my weight *up!*" Sam waved her arm at Patsi, who was on duty that night.

"I live to serve," Patsi said dryly, coming over to Sam. "But make it quick, we're short a waitress."

"A small pizza with everything," Sam ordered. "And a large Coke."

"Got it," Patsi said, and took off toward the kitchen.

Sam saw Diana near the bar, rubbing herself all over the actor William McWilliams. "Scum comes in all packages, doesn't it?" Sam mused.

"Unfortunately there are a lot of scummy people in show business," X said, sipping his drink. "It tends to attract them."

"You're not," Sam replied flirtatiously.

"Well, yeah, but I'm exceptional," X joked.

"So tell me about the jerks," Sam prompted.

X launched into a fifteen-minute monologue about some of the show business types he had met during his years as a dancer, and particularly as someone running a dance company. He had particular distaste for commercial producers.

"They'd produce an execution live if they thought it would sell tickets," he joked.

"*Death of Diana!* The new musical hit!" Sam cracked.

"That's show biz," X sighed, and looked around the Play Café.

"Getting on toward closing time," he remarked, as the crowd was beginning to thin out.

Sam saw Diana leaving with the actor, draped all over him. "I'm having too much fun to go home," Sam told X. "Feel like going for a walk?"

"Sure," X replied. "Toward the beach?"

"Why not?" Sam answered.

X got up, paid the bill, and they strolled out of the Play Café arm in arm. Together, they walked down Main Street, toward the beach. Just a few cars passed them in the still night—there was no moon, and the stars shone overhead in the clear Maine air.

I adore this guy, Sam thought to herself. *He is so different, and talented. And so laid back! There's no pressure with him. Almost any guy that I've spent this much time with has made a major effort to try to get into my pants. But not X!*

"Let's stop here," Sam suggested. They were walking past one of the municipal parks on the way to the beach. They sat down on one of the park benches, and the smell of the ocean mingled with the smell of the irises, petunias, and marigolds that were growing in beds all over the park.

"Mmmmm, smells great," X commented, inhaling deeply. He closed his eyes and savored the moment.

"I agree," Sam said, and unconsciously moved closer to X on the bench.

"We're going to make a great team, you know," X remarked.

"We already are a great team," Sam murmured.

And then she surprised herself, because Sam Bridges was someone who almost never had to make the first move with a guy. All she'd ever had to do was wait, and the guy moved on her, just like the sun coming up in the morning. With the exception of Danny Franklin, who was really just a friend anyway.

This time, though, she made the first move. She put her arm around X, touched his cheek tenderly, and kissed him on the lips.

She got a weird reaction.

She was expecting X to kiss her back.

Instead, he merely grinned. And then he actually laughed out loud.

Oh God, Sam thought, *this is totally humiliating! He's laughing at me!*

"I have bad news for you, Sam," X said.

"You're not attracted to me, it's okay," Sam said quickly. "Just forget I did that, please. Pretend it didn't happen, I—"

"Sam, I need to explain something to you—"

"Or you're involved already," Sam continued nervously. "That's it, right?"

"No, not really, but—" X admitted.

"Hey, it's cool, no biggie, honest," Sam

babbled, trying to cover her terrible embarrassment. "I just wish you'd told me about her, that's all."

X hesitated for a moment. "There is no her," he said quietly, his voice gentle. "I thought you understood."

"Understood what?" Sam asked, totally puzzled.

"Sam, I'm gay," X answered.

TWELVE

"You're gay," Sam repeated, nearly dumbfounded.

"That's right," X said.

"As in you don't like girls," Sam said.

"Oh, I like girls fine," X said easily. "I just don't have intimate relationships with them."

"I can't believe it."

"Believe it," X grinned. "They believe it in Mankato, Minnesota, though it did take them some getting used to."

"But, but, but—" Sam sputtered like a faulty outboard motor, "but why didn't you tell me before?"

X looked at her closely. "I did tell you."

"No you didn't," Sam insisted. She quickly thought back on all of the conversations they'd had together. "I'm serious, you never told me!"

"Come on, Sam," X chided her. "I told you I didn't have any plans to have children."

"So!" Sam responded. "Neither do I!"

"I told you I was the black sheep in the family. The blackest, I think is what I said."

"And I am, too!" Sam protested. "But that doesn't mean I'm gay!"

"Sam, I run a dance company. It's two plus two equals four!"

"Well, I don't think so!" Sam stated.

"You really haven't been out of Kansas for very long, have you?" X asked ironically.

"Hey, that's not fair!" Sam fumed. "I don't think I was being so naive! Plenty of guys don't want to have kids! Plenty of guys don't fit in in Minnesota! And plenty of guys who are dancers aren't gay!"

X stared at her a minute. "Maybe . . ." he finally conceded.

"Maybe is right," Sam insisted. "It's not like I could tell by looking at you!"

"It's not something that you tattoo on your arm," X said wryly.

"But . . . you don't look gay!"

Here X's face hardened for a moment. "What's that supposed to mean?" he asked.

"You don't look Jewish!"

"There's no such thing as 'looking Jewish,'" Sam shot back.

"Exactly my point," X said quietly.

"But I just never thought . . . I mean I always thought that gay guys . . ." Sam couldn't finish her sentence.

"You thought we all put on eye liner and minced down the boardwalk in drag?" X finished.

Sam blushed. *Busted,* she thought.

"Look, Sam, there are as many different kinds of gay people as there are different kinds of straight people," X said gently.

"I knew you were too good to be true," Sam said with a sigh. She kicked at the dirt below the bench where they were sitting.

"What's that supposed to mean?" X asked her.

"That you weren't all over me like white

on rice," Sam explained, using one of Pres's favorite expressions.

"Look at it this way," X suggested. "You're not used to having guys turn you down, huh?"

"No," Sam replied. "It's always me who turns them down."

"Well," X said, and here he grinned. "You can consider your record still perfect."

Sam thought about it for a moment, and then she managed a small smile. Here she was, rejected, but she didn't feel bad about it, and her record was still perfect.

"Sam!" Becky Jacobs's voice carried up the stairs of the house. "Phone for you!"

Sam opened her eyes and looked groggily at the clock. 8:45 a.m. She'd overslept, after staying in the park with X until nearly two o'clock.

"Hello?" she croaked into the phone.

"Hold one minute, please," a voice said.

Who the hell is that? Sam wondered. She closed her eyes and thought about the night before. *Wow, X told me he's gay,* she recalled. *What a shocker. I like him so much. It's going to be so great to dance with him. So why do I still have this awful feeling in my stomach? And what was I dreaming that was so intense right before Becky called to wake me up.*

And then her dream came flooding back. She had dreamed that she was on stage again at Madison Square Garden, singing with the Flirts. Emma and Diana De Witt were right next to her. And then, just like with Johnny Angel earlier in the summer, a lighting instrument had come crashing down on her.

In real life, Sam thought, *that put me in the hospital. But in my dream, it just bounced off me, and I kept on singing.*

I wonder what that's supposed to mean?

"Sam?" an unfamiliar female voice said through the phone.

"Yes, who is this?" Sam asked.

"It's Kristy Powell, from the *Breakers.*"

What's she calling me for? Sam thought.

"Hi, Kristy," Sam mumbled, still waking up.

"You have any comment?" Kristy asked.

"About what?" Sam replied, puzzled.

"I understand the Flirts are auditioning new backup singers tomorrow," Kristy responded, a trace of superciliousness in her voice. "Because of a certain backup singer who quit."

Sam got that sick feeling in her stomach again.

"They're auditioning already?" Sam asked before she could censor her question.

"Hmmm, sounds like you're upset," Kristy said, sensing some dirt for her gossip column.

"No, no, not at all," Sam lied.

"So it's true, then, that you quit," Kristy probed.

"It's more complicated than that," Sam replied.

"Well, you can tell me your side if you want to," Kristy said, "but if you don't, I can't say you're going to look very good in print."

"I guess I'll risk it," Sam snapped and hung up the phone.

Sam buried her head in her hands. *Oh, God. They're auditioning my replacement,* she thought miserably. *It's really true. I've really burned my bridges this time. Stupid Sam who-burns-her-Bridges. That's me.*

"I'm really glad you came over, Sam," Ian Templeton said to her sheepishly, as they stood in Graham Perry's palatial backyard.

"No prob," Sam replied easily, though she didn't have a clue as to why Ian had called her not twenty minutes after she'd gotten off the phone with Kristy Powell. Sam had been sure he was calling for Becky, but to her surprise he'd asked her to come over to the Templetons. Alone. Luckily, Dan had plans for the twins, so Sam had most of the morning off.

"Where's Carrie?" Sam asked, both wanting to see and dreading seeing her friend.

"She had to take Chloe to the dentist; she fell and chipped her tooth on the pool," Ian said, settling down into one of the comfortable outdoor chairs near the pool.

"Yuck," Sam replied, sitting near Ian.

Ian looked distinctly uncomfortable, but he didn't say anything.

"So, what's up?" Sam finally asked, sitting down near him.

"Well, uh . . ." Ian began, biting nervously at a hangnail. "I . . . uh . . . there was something I wanted to talk to you about. I don't want to talk to Mom and Dad."

"Why don't you talk to Carrie?" Sam suggested, amazed that Ian didn't want to confide in his level-headed au pair, and instead was choosing her to share some big secret.

"Well, I could," Ian said, "but it's about—you know—girls and stuff. So I thought I should ask you."

First Becky, now Ian, Sam thought. *If all else fails I'll chuck all this show biz stuff and start a column for the lovelorn.*

"Carrie is really smart, you know," Sam said. "I don't feel like I can give anyone very good advice right about now."

"Yeah, I know she's smart," Ian agreed. He reached over and picked up a couple of pebbles to shake nervously in his hand. "But, see, I figured you're more experienced."

Sam snickered quietly, and then coughed

to cover it up. *Things aren't always what they seem. If people knew that I'm still a virgin, and Carrie isn't, they'd never believe it.*

"So, what's on your mind?" Sam asked.

"I wanted to talk to you about Becky," Ian said solemnly, shaking his pebbles together.

"Uh-huh," Sam agreed.

"Well, I kinda think maybe she likes me," Ian mumbled.

"Uh-huh," Sam agreed.

"And I kinda, well, I sorta always liked her," Ian admitted. He looked over at Sam. "Do you think she likes me?"

"Yep," Sam replied confidently.

"Really?" Ian asked eagerly. "How do you know?"

"I just do," Sam said with a shrug. "You want me to keep this talk secret, right?"

Ian nodded.

"Then you'll have to respect what I know, if you understand what I'm saying," Sam said. She turned her chair so that it better faced the sun.

"Wow, that means she told you," Ian ventured.

"Would that be good?" Sam asked him.

"I guess," Ian said. "But here's the thing. Last summer, when I liked her a lot, she treated me like dogmeat."

"So," Sam said thoughtfully, thinking about the dream she had the night before, "people can change."

"Not Becky!"

"Even Becky," Sam said.

"Yeah, but what if she only likes me because my dad is famous?" Ian asked, looking miserable.

"Nope, not the case," Sam reported. "I think she likes you because she thinks of you as an artist."

Ian's face lit up. "No kidding?"

"No kidding."

"Wow," Ian breathed. Then his face grew cloudy again. "Yeah, but here's another thing. I think the only reason she likes me now is because I don't act like I like her."

Sam looked over at Ian. "You're telling me you do like her but you act like you don't like her."

"Right," Ian agreed.

"So why do you do that?" Sam wondered.

"Because the less attention I pay to her, the more attention she pays to me," Ian responded. "Wait a sec. You want a soda?"

Sam nodded. Ian disappeared into the house for a moment, and came out holding two cans of 7UP. He handed one to Sam, who took it gratefully, popped it open, and took a big swig. Ian stared at Sam expectantly.

"So you really like her?" Sam asked, trying to jump-start the conversation again.

"Becky?" Ian asked, blushing to even say her name.

No, Madonna, Sam was tempted to say.

"Yep," Sam replied.

"Well," Ian said, taking a sip of soda. "I like her a lot. Really a lot."

"So what's the biggie?" Sam asked lightly. "You like her, she likes you—"

"Don't you see?" Ian asked. "Now that I'm ignoring her, she's paying attention to me. I'm afraid that if I pay attention to her, she'll ignore me."

"Why would she do a dumb thing like that?" Sam asked.

"She did last summer," Ian sniffed.

"Ian, I've been trying to tell you," Sam said patiently, "Becky is not stuck in a time-warp. She's growing up. She likes you. She really, really likes you. Not because you're Graham Perry's son, and not because you've been ignoring her."

"Honest?" Ian asked, hope radiating across his face.

"Ian, you're so scared of her turning you down that you're not letting yourself have the fun of having her like you!" Sam exclaimed.

"Yeah, that's right," Ian said, thoughtfully.

"So, what's the worst thing that could happen if she rejects you?"

"I'd be bummed out," Ian replied, truthfully.

"That's true."

"I'd be totally humiliated in front of the band," he added.

"Worth the risk," Sam replied. "And what if instead you didn't let Becky know you liked her—she'd think you were rejecting *her*."

"And Allie would probably get a crush on me. Because if Becky can't have something, Allie wants it," Ian reasoned.

Sam burst out laughing. "Listen, Ian, when you really like someone, the best thing to do is to be honest about it."

"But, you know, it's kind of like, scary," Ian said with a shrug. He dented in his empty soda can.

"I know," Sam agreed. "But if you reject someone just because you're afraid they might reject you first, you'll never end up with that person! You'll never get what you want!"

Ian smiled shyly at Sam, and Sam smiled back.

But she wasn't really thinking about Ian. She was thinking about Pres, and Danny, and The Flirts. She was thinking about how very afraid she was that she'd be rejected, so afraid that she'd rejected everyone and everything first.

I must be the biggest fool in the world, Sam thought. *Because I just gave Ian the advice that I've been too stupid to give to myself.*

*　*　*

Sam drove back to the Jacobs house, her mind going a thousand miles an hour.

It's so obvious, she thought. *How could I have been so stupid? So blind?*

Sam thought it through, to make sure that she wasn't jumping to conclusions.

She thought so hard that she paid less attention to her driving than she should have, and just missed running a red light. A car honked at her, startling her. Adrenaline rushed through her veins.

Concentrate on one thing at a time, she told herself, gripping the steering wheel hard. But all the way back to the Jacobses, all she could think was how dumb she'd been. How incredibly dumb.

She parked in the driveway and stared off into the distance. *The advice I gave to Ian is the right advice for me*, she thought. *He's not the only one who's afraid of being rejected. I cut out of the band because I was afraid of being humiliated by Billy because of my singing. I never let Pres get close to me because I was afraid he'd reject me. I used Danny to stop myself from get-*

ting close to Pres, and then I got so afraid of Danny rejecting me that I pushed him away too.

"I could lose everything, everyone," Sam whispered, tears coming to her eyes, "just because I'm so afraid."

It was like a light bulb had gone off in her head. She thought back again to her dream of the night before. In the dream, the lighting instrument had hit her on the head. It should have injured her, but she stayed right on stage, singing, unhurt.

It doesn't have to be this way, Sam told herself. *I don't have to do it this way. I can find another way. I know I can!*

"Oh, please," she prayed out loud, "please. Don't let it be too late."

THIRTEEN

"So, have you recovered from my big announcement last night?" X asked Sam as they walked along the boardwalk. "Or did you call to tell me I should be locked away from decent people forever and ever, amen."

"Very funny," Sam replied. The wind whipped some hair into her face and she pushed it behind her ear.

"I take it you didn't call me to try and talk me into being straight?" X asked ironically.

Sam looked over at him. "Is that possible?"

"Nope," X said. He reached down and picked up a pink, translucent seashell and threw it toward the ocean. "You can't recruit someone to be straight any more than you can recruit someone to be gay. It's one of those myths a lot of misguided people believe."

They walked along slowly in companionable silence for a while, but Sam felt tense and anxious. She had so much on her mind, so many wrongs she felt like she needed to right.

"Listen, I take it you have something on your mind," X finally said. "This doesn't feel like a simple stroll down the beach."

"I guess it's not," Sam agreed. "I just don't know where . . . how to begin."

"At the beginning," X suggested.

Sam sighed and stared out at the ocean. Then she told X everything—about Pres, about Danny, about her real reason for quitting the Flirts. "I have been the biggest idiot of all time," she finally concluded.

"Yeah, you're right up there," X agreed.

Sam turned to him with tears in her eyes.

"I'm teasing you," he said gently, putting his arm around her shoulders.

They started walking again. "The Flirts

are holding auditions for my replacement today," Sam said miserably. "It hurts so much."

"Well, maybe it's not too late," X said thoughtfully.

"But it is," Sam insisted. "They all hate me. I let them down, I ran out on them."

"So run back in on them," X said. "Go to the audition."

"And what?" Sam asked. "What do you mean?"

"And audition," X said simply.

Sam stood stock-still. *Could I really do that?* she asked herself. *What if I'm totally humiliated and they don't want me—I couldn't stand that. But wait, that's the kind of thinking that got me into this situation in the first place!*

"X," she said, "What about us?"

"Fred and Ginger?" X asked lightly.

"I love dancing with you," Sam said passionately. "I love it more than anything I've ever done in my life."

X grinned at her. "Yeah, we are pretty terrif together," he agreed. "But it sounds like you left the Flirts for all the wrong reasons. And until you go make that right, you can't be right for anything else."

"What if they don't want me?" Sam whispered.

"Well, Sam, I guess this time that is a chance you are just going to have to take," X replied.

"Will we still be friends?" Sam asked him, a lump in her throat.

"You have a new lifelong buddy," X assured her. "And if the Flirts won't take you back, we will dance off into the sunset together."

Sam turned to X and gave him a huge hug. "You are the greatest."

The looked at each other and grinned, and then they both said: "Hey, to know me is to love me!"

Sam laughed, then she grew more solemn. "I don't suppose you have any wise advice for me about guys, do you?"

"I could probably use some wise advice along those lines myself," X responded. "I'll try, though. Which guy do you dream about?"

Sam thought a minute. "Pres," she admitted. "But I love Danny! I feel like . . . well, like I feel when I'm with you, you know? Comfortable!"

X raised his eyebrows at Sam. "Very telling."

"It is?"

"Um-hum," X said. "No sexual vibes with Danny, is what you're saying. You love Danny like a friend."

"But he's so perfect for me!" Sam protested. "Pres is scarier. He makes me feel like I could . . . I don't know . . . do something stupid—"

"Walk off a cliff?" X suggested. "Skydive without a parachute? Risk being hurt?"

"Yes!" Sam exclaimed. "I don't feel in control with Pres, and it's so scary! I'm afraid I'll want to—"

"Make love with him?" X asked.

Sam nodded. "I'm scared of that most of all."

"Love is not supposed to be scary," X replied. "At least that's what I've heard. Anyway, you can risk it, or not. It's your choice."

197

"No pain, no gain?" Sam asked with a sigh.

"Something like that," X agreed. "Maybe it's not sex you're afraid of so much as it is how close that might make you and Pres."

"Why would I be afraid of that?" Sam wondered.

"Who knows why people are so afraid of intimacy?" X asked with a shrug. "If I knew the answer to that I'd write a how-to book, do the talk show circuit, and make a mint."

Sam looked at her watch. "The auditions are in an hour at the Play Café. I read it in the paper this morning."

"Are you going to risk it?" X asked.

"Do you really think I should?"

"The question, Sam, is do *you* really think you should," X asked gently.

Sam hesitated. "I do," she finally said.

"Well, then, go get 'em!" He held up crossed fingers and smiled at Sam.

She hugged him one more time. "I love you, X," she whispered fiercely, and ran back to the car.

BACKUP AUDITIONS FOR THE FLIRTS—TO-DAY, 1:00, the sign on the door of the Play Café read.

Sam walked up to the door and took a deep, ragged breath. Her hands were shaking so hard she could barely hold her purse.

Run away! a voice in her head told her. *You don't have to put yourself through this!*

"Oh yes, you do," she said out loud, hoping the very sound of her voice would give her some courage. With another deep breath, she pulled open the door of the cafe.

Once her eyes adjusted to the light, Sam saw a cluster of about twenty girls near the stage. To the right she saw Jay, Sly, Billy, and Pres. Pres. Her heart leaped in her chest. He looked so gorgeous and she missed him so much. To the left of the stage she saw Diana and Emma. They were wearing leotards and tights and were talking quietly to each other. Carrie was there, too, roaming around snapping candid shots of the auditioners.

I'm the outsider now, Sam realized. *I'm not a part of them anymore.*

Diana stood up and got everyone's attention. "Everyone who is auditioning needs to have signed in on this sheet," she said imperiously. She held up a sheet of paper. "If your name is not here, you don't audition. Is there anyone who didn't sign in?"

Sam took a few steps forward into the light. "Me," she said.

Everyone turned and stared at her. There was silence in the room.

"Yeah, very hilarious," Diana finally said. She turned her attention from Sam. "Okay, we got everyone? Make sure you have a number and—"

"I don't have a number," Sam insisted, holding her ground. "I'm here to audition."

Once again everyone stared at her. Finally Emma walked over to Sam.

"Sam?" she asked.

"I mean it," Sam whispered to Emma, scared she was going to fall over, pass out, or die. But she didn't. "I want to audition for my spot."

"But . . . but you quit," Emma said.

"And it was the stupidest thing I ever did in my life," Sam told her earnestly. "And I'm asking for a second chance."

Emma hesitated a second, then she smiled and reached for Sam's hand. She led Sam closer to the stage. "Sam is here to audition," she told everyone in a firm voice.

"Yes!" Carrie exclaimed enthusiastically. She ran over to Sam and hugged her hard.

Sam hugged her back. *Emma and Carrie are the two best friends anyone ever had,* Sam thought. *They really, really care about me.* Knowing that gave her the courage to turn to the guys in the band. "Can I?" she asked them, deliberately not looking Pres in the eye. "Can I audition?"

"Give me a major break here!" Diana fumed, marching over to the band. "Do you believe this bimbo? One day she quits, the next day she wants back in? And she can't even sing!"

"All I want is a chance," Sam said, forcing her voice to remain steady. "I'll audition with everyone else."

"Oh yeah, real fair," a girl in the crowd mumbled.

Billy walked over to Sam. "What kind of game are you pulling now?" he asked her in a low voice.

"No game," Sam insisted. "I made a big mistake, Billy. And I'm really, really sorry. And I want a chance to make things right again."

"You messed up, then you couldn't take the heat, then you ran out on us," Billy whispered in a harsh voice. "Why should we trust you again?"

"Maybe you shouldn't," Sam admitted. "I don't know if I'd trust me, if I were in your position." Sam held her head high and willed herself not to cry in front of all these people.

Carrie came over to Billy and put her hand on his arm. "Billy, please," she said earnestly. "Please, give her a chance."

Billy stared at Sam a moment longer, then he went to consult with the guys in the band.

Diana sauntered over to Sam and looked her over, head to toe, then back up again.

"Gee, you look like the same no-talent quitter you looked like a few days ago,"

"Shut up, Diana," Emma snapped.

"Why should I?" Diana barked back at Emma. "I don't have to put up with this!" She turned on Sam. "What happened, did X turn you down?"

"No," Sam said steadily.

"I'll have you know X wants me bad," Diana continued coolly. "In fact, he made a huge play for me. He is hot—very hot."

Sam bit her lip to keep from laughing. "Is that so?"

"Yes," Diana replied. "He calls me to ask me out all the time. So I guess I'll be dividing my time between X and Pres—something you weren't exactly able to handle."

"No, I wasn't," Sam agreed. She looked over at Emma and Carrie. Sometime she was going to have to tell them about X being gay so they'd appreciate how funny Diana's lies were.

"Okay, Sam," Billy said, walking back over to her. "We've decided to let you audition."

"Oh, thank you!" Sam cried.

"But that's all," Billy warned. "You won't get any preferential treatment."

"I'm not asking for any," Sam assured him.

"Hold on a red-hot minute!" Diana exploded. "This is crazy! She can't even sing! Everyone knows we're better off without her!"

"Chill out, Diana," Billy suggested. "We've made a decision."

Everyone turned away from Diana.

"Oh, okay, fine, be that way," Diana snapped. "Let me know how everything turns out. Suddenly I feel too sick to stay." She picked up her dance bag and slammed out the door.

"See, this is why I never wanted girls in the band," Sly groused, slapping his fist on the table.

"Let's just get started," Billy said wearily. He picked up the audition list. "Can I have number one on stage? Beth Merriwhether?"

A short girl with curly blonde hair went up on stage. She conferred with Jay at the piano, then she came center.

"I'm singing 'You Take My Breath Away,'" she told the band nervously. Then she launched into the song Billy had written for Carrie.

Sam sat with Emma and Carrie, nervous sweat pouring off her. Girl after girl went up to sing. Some were awful, some were okay, a couple were really good.

I can sing, Sam told herself steadily as she watched the auditions. *I can*.

Finally all the auditioners had sung except Sam.

"Sam, you're on," Billy called to her.

Slowly, Sam went up on stage. She had no earthly idea what she should sing. And then it popped into her head. She walked over to Jay, whispered something, and took center stage. And she sang.

Sometimes I feel like a motherless
   child.
Sometimes I feel like a motherless
   child.
Sometimes I feel like a motherless
   child.
A long, long way from my home.

It was an old spiritual, the same one Emma had sung for her audition months earlier. And as Sam sang, tears ran down her cheeks. Because some distant knowledge was beginning to creep into her mind. What she was singing was true. She did feel like a motherless child. She felt like the mother who had raised her and who had never told her she was adopted wasn't really her mother, nor was the birth mother who had given her away. And something about feeling that both those women had rejected her in some deep, fundamental way made Sam afraid to really, fully love or trust anyone.

A long, long way from my home.

Sam finished singing, and there was a hush in the cafe. Then Emma and Carrie were standing up, applauding wildly, grinning up at Sam. A few other girls joined halfheartedly in the applause, some others just looked bummed out.

Sam came down from the stage and walked over to Emma and Carrie. They both threw their arms around her at once.

"Oh-mi-God!" Carrie yelled, "you were so wonderful! That's the best I ever heard you sing!"

"Me, too!" Emma added happily.

Sam looked at her two best friends. "Thanks," she said gruffly. "Whatever happens, I want you guys to know how sorry I am that I . . . that I let you down. I'm really, really sorry."

"Hey, we're the Three Musketeers," Carrie reminded Sam, tears swimming in her eyes.

"No matter what the guys decide," Emma said fervently. "Oh, Sam, we missed you so much!"

Billy finished talking with the band, and then he jumped up on stage. "I want to thank you all for auditioning. Normally we'd have dance callbacks tomorrow, but under the circumstances that won't be necessary." His eyes found Sam's. "We already know you can dance," he told her.

Carrie and Emma turned to Sam, then they both screamed.

"You're in! You're in!" they screamed, hugging her and jumping up and down.

"This was fixed, if you ask me," a girl hissed to her friend.

"What a waste of time," someone else said with disgust.

Sam looked across the room and saw Pres sitting alone at a small table. *I have to face him,* she told herself. *I have to risk it.* "Excuse me," she told her friends, and walked over to Pres.

"Hi," she said softly.

"Hey," Pres answered.

She sat down next to him. "Thank you for letting me back in the band. It means everything to me."

Pres gave Sam a steady look. "I'll tell you the truth, Sam. I didn't vote for you."

Sam's heart turned over. "You . . . you didn't?"

"Nope," Pres said. "I think you have some growin' up to do. I didn't think we should chance it. I was outvoted."

"Oh," Sam said softly. She stared at her hands a moment. "I've done a lot of thinking, Pres. You're right, I've been acting like a spoiled brat for a long time. But . . . but I think I'm changing."

"Well, that's good, Sam," Pres replied.

She took a deep breath. It was now or never. "I miss you," she whispered. "I miss you so much. And I want you back."

It seemed forever that her confession hung in the air, forever before Pres opened his mouth.

"I miss you, too," Pres admitted.

"Really?" Sam cried, hope filling her heart. "Oh, Pres, I—"

"But it won't work, Sam," Pres continued, cutting her off. "I just can't go through it with you again."

"But it wouldn't be like before!" Sam protested.

Pain filled Pres's eyes. "How can I know that, Sam? You talk the talk but you don't walk the walk. I just can't go back."

"We wouldn't, we'd go forward," Sam insisted. "Pres . . . I . . . I love you," she whispered.

"You just think you love me because you lost me," Pres said sadly.

"No, that's not true—"

"It's over, Sam," Pres said quietly.

Feeling as if her heart were breaking, Sam watched Pres pick up his jean jacket and walk out the door. Tears streamed down her face. She couldn't move.

"Sam?" Emma asked, coming up next to her.

"I lost him," Sam whispered. "I've lost him forever."

Carrie came up on the other side of her. "Maybe not forever," she said gently.

Sam turned her tear-stained face to Carrie. "Do you think there's hope? Any hope at all?"

"Well, you'll be in the band together," Carrie said. "Maybe if he sees you've really changed, maybe . . ."

"I will show him," Sam said passionately. She looked at her friends. "Why is it that you don't appreciate what you have until it's gone?"

"I don't know, Sam," Emma said with a sigh. "I wish I did."

"There's so much I have to tell you guys," Sam said earnestly, "so many things about myself I'm just beginning to figure out."

She wiped the tears off her face with the back of her hand. "Why does it have to be so tough just to grow up?"

"I don't know the answer to that one, either," Emma said with a small smile.

"At least we have each other," Carrie reminded them.

"Always," Emma said fervently.

"You guys are everything," Sam told them. She looked toward the door and pictured Pres walking away. Maybe, with time, she'd be able to convince Pres that she really had changed, that she was ready to be vulnerable, to take risks. She knew now how much she loved Pres, and she knew she had to tell Danny the truth, even though it would hurt him.

"I love Danny like you love Josh," Sam realized, turning to Carrie.

"Then you have to tell him so," Carrie said.

"I know," Sam replied. "I'm going to." She made a mental note to write him a long letter telling him just how much his friendship meant to her.

Then she realized something else. "You

know, it's funny—Pres dropped me, and I have to drop Danny, and X is . . . well, I'll explain about X sometime . . . but Sam Bridges is about to have zero guys in her life."

"Sam, you don't have to have a guy," Emma pointed out.

"I . . . I guess that's right," Sam replied. "But it feels so . . . weird."

"It might just be good for you," Carrie said.

"I hate stuff that's good for me," Sam protested. "And I still want Pres."

Emma and Carrie gave her looks of disgust.

"Well, I can't turn over a totally new leaf—you wouldn't even recognize me!" Sam exclaimed. A small smile came to her lips. "But I'm trying. I'm really, really trying."

Emma and Carrie smiled back at her.

They couldn't ask for anything more.

SUNSET ISLAND MAILBOX

Dear Readers,

I hope you're not sick of hearing how great your letters are, because I just have to tell you again. I have learned so much from you: what you like, what you want to read about, what you really care about. And I try to bring all of that into every Sunset book.

Special thanks to Jessica Dimmet, Amber Lawrence and Amanda Braun of Sebastopol, California, who sent me the greatest photo to prove that the three of them really do look like Sam, Emma and Carrie. You guys are the cutest! And to Sara Plantan of Peru, Illinois, and her friend at cheerleading camp—I loved the photo of the two of you holding up Sunset books!

Recently I got a truly incredible letter. It's so unique that I just have to share the whole thing with you. Once you've read it, you'll see what I mean. If the red unit of the Ringling Brothers Barnum and Bailey Circus comes to your town, look up Getty, your sister Sunset Island fan!

As always, I answer each and every letter I receive. Just let me know if you want a personal response only, or if I can consider your letter for publication.

Thanks for being the greatest readers in the world!

See you on the island!
Best —
Cherie Bennett

Cherie Bennett
c/o General Licensing Company
24 West 25th Street
New York, New York 10010

All letters printed become property of the publisher.

Hi, Cherie,
My name is Getty. I'm fifteen, and I come from Europe, Bulgaria. I'm here with my sister performing with the Ringling Brothers Barnum and Bailey Circus. We both do a great Hula Hoop act, teeter board act, and perch pole act. I ride the elephants and my sister goes into a big metal globe and three motorcycles ride around her. Pretty cool, huh?
Before we got to America, my family and I traveled all over Europe to different circuses and we got a contract here. I spoke very little

English in the beginning but now I'm getting better.

About two months ago I started reading your Sunset Island books. I think they're great. I can't even put them down, they are so good. I love to read them!

Life in the circus is great. I was born into it and I'll always stay with it. My family has been in the circus for generations. You can find us in the 1987 Guiness Book of World Records *for doing a seven-man-high pyramid while a person does a backflip and lands all the way on top. I'm the fifth person on the pyramid.*

You are welcome to see our show anytime we're in town. Make sure you ask for me and make sure it's the red unit because there are two units.

That's about it. Please don't forget to write me back.

God bless, your new friend,

Getty

P.S. Cherie, your name in Bulgarian is Zepu Behet.

> *Getty Kehaiova*
> *Ringling Brothers Barnum*
> *and Bailey Circus*

439